MARCEL SCHWOB

THE ASSASSINS
AND OTHER STORIES

TRANSLATED
AND WITH AN INTRODUCTION BY
SUE BOSWELL

THIS IS A SNUGGLY BOOK

Translation and Introduction Copyright © 2020
by Sue Boswell.

ISBN: 978-1-64525-036-4

THE ASSASSINS
AND OTHER STORIES

MARCEL SCHWOB (1867-1905) was sent to Paris in 1881 to study at the Lycée Louis-le-Grand, where he met the future writers Léon Daudet and Paul Claudel; he lived with his uncle, the novelist Léon Cahun. He became a professional journalist in 1888, working on both *L'Événement* and *L'Écho de Paris*. His great admiration for Edgar Poe is very obvious in his story collections *Coeur double* (Ollendorf 1891) and *Le Roi au masque d'or* (1892), translations from which can be found in the sampler *The King in the Golden Mask* (Carcanet, 1985). Other works exhibiting a strong Symbolist influence include the quasi-autobiographical *Le Livre de Monelle* (1894) and a book of fictitious biographies, *Vies imaginaires* (1896), but his health deteriorated catastrophically as a result of an undiagnosable chronic condition, which eventually killed him.

SUE BOSWELL studied French Language and Literature at UCL and for a time taught French at Goldsmiths University of London. She then moved into university administration, specialising in university external relations and communications. Later she became a translator for the Wiener Library for the study of the Holocaust and Genocide. Her translations include *The Last Train* by Arnaud Rykner (Snuggly Books, 2020).

Contents

Introduction

MARCEL SCHWOB was like a shooting star who flashed across the French literary firmament at the end of the nineteenth century. In his relatively short life (1867-1905) he was a friend of or associated with nearly all the most important literary and artistic figures in France at that time (Paul Claudel, Paul Verlaine, Octave Mirbeau, Guillaume Apollinaire, Henri Barbusse, Paul Valéry, Aristide Bruant, Marcel Proust, Edouard Manet, August Rodin and Camille Claudel). But his literary friendships were not restricted to France, as he was also close to the Belgian writer Maurice Maeterlinck and to the British authors Robert Louis Stevenson and Oscar Wilde, whose *Salome* Schwob translated into French. The strength of some of these friendships is shown by the fact that Paul Valéry dedicated two works to him, that Alfred Jarry dedicated *Ubu Roi* to him, and that Oscar Wilde dedicated the long poem *The Sphynx* to him.

And yet today, when one asks well-read French people about late nineteenth-century French literature, they become animated when one mentions Flaubert,

Zola, and Maupassant, but often seem perplexed when the name Marcel Schwob is raised. The German poet Rilke had the same reaction when he read the German translation of Schwob's *La Croisade des Enfants* (tr. as *The Children's Crusade*), which was published in France in 1896 and with its first German translation in 1902. Rilke claimed to have read the novella twice over, to have been profoundly moved, and to have been amazed that he had never heard the name of Marcel Schwob, asking himself, "Who is he?"

One hopes that the publication in English of this collection of some of Marcel Schwob's work, *The Assassins and other Stories*, will bring this neglected author to the further attention of an English-speaking audience. These stories will surprise and at times mystify those readers who are used to the nineteenth-century French tradition from Prosper Mérimée (*Carmen*) and culminating in the realistic even naturalistic stories of Guy de Maupassant, with strong narrative lines but also with twists in the plot to catch out the reader as in "La Parure" (tr. as "The Necklace"), for example, in which the wife of a humble, mid-ranking civil servant borrows a precious necklace from a friend so as to be able to attend a prestigious ball. She of course loses the necklace, replaces it, spends years in drudgery paying off the debt only to be told at the end by the necklace's owner that it was in fact a fake. Marcel Schwob was no realist or naturalist. He was arguably a symbolist and possibly a precursor of surrealism. But in his stories he inevitably must use one of the short story-teller's standard devices, that of picking on a significant detail to shorten the narrative. In "The Necklace" Maupassant chooses a tablecloth that has been in use for three days to reveal the frustration of the civil servant's wife and her disappointment with her straitened circumstances. In the story "Articles for Export" Marcel Schwob has a character ask, "Are the inhabitants not whole people?" in response to the publisher's statistics about magazine subscriptions and this is all we need to know about his naïvety.

The breadth of subject matter and themes in the present volume reveals the erudition of the author. At the age of eleven he had encountered the work of Edgar Allan Poe in Baudelaire's translation. He became fluent in English and German and knew Latin. He studied philology and Sanskrit under Ferdinand de Saussure, who was later to become the forefather of Structuralism. He became fascinated by the slang used by the fifteenth-century writer Villon and co-authored a slang dictionary. Schwob refers to Poe as well as to Eugène Sue, Aristide Bruant and Balzac. In "The Execution" the poet Rodolphe Darzens appears as an onlooker and there are also references to Dostoyevsky and to Turgenev. There is a comparison in "Possessed by the Devil" between a scene in the short story and one in Defoe's *Moll Flanders*.

In this collection the stories are presented in the chronological order of their publication, beginning with the fragments "Poupa" (1883-1886), sketches from a project for a novel set in Latin antiquity, through to "The Life of Morphiel" (1895) and "Towards Utopia", unpublished at the time of Schwob's death in 1905. The subject matter covers a much wider spread of time. In "Rampsinit" we are taken back to Egyptian antiquity. Schwob's father had spent ten years in Egypt in the diplomatic service. One story, "The Life of Morphiel", takes the reader into the Platonic view of the creation of the world according to the gnostic system. "Poupa" and "The Tiber's Nuptials" are set in Rome, although the latter is based on a legend about the "marriage" of the rivers Tiber and Nera. Schwob reveals to us his knowledge of medieval European history in the two stories set in Switzerland, "The 'Reds' in Basle (1430)" and "Nidau". One story, "Blackbeard", is a racy pirate story set in the Caribbean in the eighteenth century. The evocation of Polynesia in "Articles for Export" and "Ancestry" echoes Schwob's journey to Samoa in search of R L Stevenson's tomb. It is not entirely clear when and where "The Hand of Glory" is set but it seems to be a contemporary Gothic horror tale set possibly in Scotland. The remaining nine stories are set, or appear to be set, in nineteenth-century France.

A fairly constant theme is one of decadence. The most striking example is clearly "The Gold Hatpin" which has as its central theme that of necrophilia. It is the most chilling of all the stories in this collection although "The Assassins", an examination of mindless violence and killing, runs it close. This story is based on contemporary events and links to the next story "The Execution" although the murder for which Eyraud is executed is not one committed in "The Assassins". In the final paragraph of "The Execution" the narrator, who may or may not be Schwob, wonders whether in coming centuries capital punishment may not come to be seen as barbaric. In this his narrator foreshadows Albert Camus both in *L'Etranger* (tr. as *The Stranger*) and in "Réflexions sur la guillotine" (tr. as "Reflections on the Guillotine"). In "The Psychology of the Three-Card Trick" Schwob takes us into the underworld of the confidence trickster. The story is one of the most inventive in the collection in its linguistic playfulness. But it also has a fascinating theme. Could the trickster succeed if the "mark", the target for the trickster, was not also out for something for nothing? A couple of rather second-rate thieves are the central characters of "Pale-Hands". Their dialogue, conducted mainly in criminal slang, is funny. But as it goes round and round in circles it seems almost a precursor of that of Vladimir and Estragon in Beckett's *En attendant Godot* (tr. as *Waiting for Godot*). Linked to the theme of decadence is that of leprosy, which is a significant strand in "Ancestry" but also appears in "Poupa" and in "The Maison Close". Leprosy is a powerful metaphor for the theme of social exclusion. Schwob uses a different macabre theme in three of the stories ("The Gold Hatpin", "The Hand of Glory" and in "The Maison Close") where he concentrates on the hand of a corpse, including that of an executed person.

The realists and naturalists normally used the third-person omniscient narrator and no longer felt it necessary to underline the veracity of their tales as does Prosper Mérimée in *Carmen* where the narrator meets a down-and-out man in a tavern who tells him his life story. Marcel Schwob has no hesitation in using a first-person narrative. In some cases, for example in "Blackbeard" and "Ancestry", the narrator is manifestly not Schwob himself. This is also the case with "The Hand of Glory" which is the deposition of a kitchen hand called Nancy. Schwob claims that "On Umbrellas" is taken from the diary of a close friend. Whoever this was, he was clearly a great anglophile with his reference to "the Oxford fellows, especially those of the lovely Balliol College". In "The Maison Close" we have a first-person plural narrator but with no indication of who "we" are.

Perhaps the most interesting of the stories from the point of view of narrative technique is "Towards Utopia". It is a third-person narrative but the characterisation of Cyprien d'Anarque, in particular his attitudes to literature and art, has aspects that make the reader think of Marcel Schwob himself. "For a while Cyprien was satisfied with his distinctiveness; but as he went on reading he had found, here and there, and written long before, certain of his own thoughts, his sentences and even his most outrageous eccentricities. So that he decided that in writing there is always imitation, even if we don't realise it." The story then moves on to a discussion of the freedom of the individual that might be seen as a premonition of existentialism.

Schwob is prepared to transfer the narrative to inanimate objects and this is particularly seen in "On Umbrellas" where the segments are told from the point of view of the different umbrellas, which are given characteristics, such snobbery or "a strange liking for dampness". In "Poupa" Schwob describes the oppressive midday heat thus: "Everything dozed in the midday silence; not even the leaves stirred . . ."; and of the house in "The Maison Close": "its windows seeming to blink as it settled to sleep."

The stories in the present collection were mainly published in periodicals. But Marcel Schwob was such a polymath that one feels almost sure that, had he lived and written in the twenty-first century, he would have been adept at electronic publishing. And therefore it is only slightly tongue in cheek that one suggests that he might have published these stories as blogs and that what you are about to read could be re-titled *Schwob's Blogs*.

With grateful thanks to Dr Colin Boswell, Dr Ken George, Dr François Calvet and Philippe Abraham for their help in preparing this translation.

—Sue Boswell

A Note on the Texts

"Poupa" consists of fragments written during the years 1883-86 as part of the project for a novel by M Schwob which was never completed; they were not published during his lifetime and first appeared in Volume 1 of his complete works published by F. Bernouard, Paris, 1927-30.

"The Gold Hatpin" was first published as "L'Épingle d'or" in *L'Écho de Paris* on May 18, 1889.

"The Psychology of the Three-card Trick" was first published as "La Psychologie du Bonneteau" in *L'Écho de Paris* on August 17, 1890.

"The Tiber's Nuptials" was first published as "Les Noces du Tibre" in *L'Écho de Paris* on December 28 ,1890.

"The Assassins" was first published as "Les Assassins" in *L'Événement* on January 26, 1891.

"The Execution" was first published as "L'Éxécution" in *L'Événement* on February 5, 1891.

"Articles for Export" was first published as "Articles d'exportation" in *Le Messager français* on March 8, 1891; it was republished with some amendments under the title "La Gloire" in *La Revue franco-américaine* in July 1895.

"On Umbrellas" was first published as "Essai sur le parapluie" in *L'Écho de Paris* on May 10, 1891.

"Pale-Hands" was first published as "Blanches-Mains" in *L'Écho de Paris* on June 19, 1892.

"Possessed by the Devil" was first published as "La Démoniaque" in *L'Écho de Paris* on July 31, 1892.

"Blackbeard" was first published as "Barbe-Noire" in *L'Écho de Paris* on October 26, 1892.

"The 'Reds' in Basle (1430)" was first published as "Les 'Rouges' à Bâle (1430)" in *L'Écho de Paris* on February 17, 1893.

"Nidau" was first published in *L'Écho de Paris* on February 25, 1893.

"The Hand of Glory" was first published as "La Main de gloire" in *L'Écho de Paris* on March 11, 1893.

"Rampsinit" was first published in *L'Écho de Paris* on March 25, 1893.

"Ancestry" was first published as "L'Origine" in *L'Écho de Paris* on May 6, 1893.

"The Maison Close" was first published as "La Maison close" in *L'Écho de Paris* on September 9, 1893.

"The Life of Morphiel" was first published as "Vie de Morphiel démiurge" in *Le Journal* on June 22, 1895.

"Towards Utopia", originally "Dialogues d'utopie", was not published during the lifetime of M Schwob; the manuscript was preserved in the municipal library of Nantes.

THE ASSASSINS
AND OTHER STORIES

Poupa

POUPA was lying beneath the trees alongside the river Nar[1]. The water flowed silently below the latticework of branches, and the sun, shining through in places, drenched the dark turf with great pools of light. She was stretched out on her back thinking, her black hair loose, her hands behind her head, and Strenou, the big mountain dog, lying flat on the ground, was licking her hands. She stayed this way for hours, saying nothing, watching the buzzing insects, the unpredictable circles of mosquitoes in the sunlight, and the water spiders scuttling along the shallow pools.

The river wound around the meadow, with the mountain rising immediately behind, green at its base and brown at the top. A path encircled it like a black bootlace; here and there thatched roofs appeared on its lower half—and higher up green broom and burnt grasses. The mountain sides were covered in oaks and tall ferns; they came down as far as the Nar, the thirsty plants leaning over to drink from it. Everything dozed

---

1 Nera in modern Italian.

in the midday silence; not even the leaves stirred. The heat weighed heavily on the wood and through the branches the shimmering of the brown mountain was too dazzling to behold.

Poupa looked as if she was deep in contemplation, but she was not thinking about anything very much. She thought of the flying insect, the scuttling spider; she laughed when Strenou tickled her or licked her too hard.

She spent all her days this way, doing nothing; or she would weave a cage to catch cicadas. It was the only thing she knew how to do. And why would she need to know more? There was the little shepherd boy Roufou to watch the sheep—and mother Mannia to look after the house. Father Variou was in the fields—sweating over his plough and his cattle, and grandfather Couprou basked in the sun on his bench, near the house. He'd lived like this for ten years—he couldn't remember anything—all he knew was eating and sleeping.

For Poupa wasn't involved—she ate so little! She was everyone's favourite. Variou himself took her on his knee when he came in from the fields, and passed his big calloused hands through her hair—making her jump.

Hey ho! Hey ho! Hop! Hop! Hop! Then old Couprou laughed his old man's laugh, understanding nothing. Once they'd seen him talking to Strenou, stroking his head: but his words had no meaning. He often laughed for hours, sitting in the sun, in front of his house.

Poupa didn't think about all that: nothing could surprise her there—she lived amongst these people, she didn't know any other life.

The house was not by the Nar. Its back was to the mountain, behind the wood which bordered the river. The roof was of thatch, the walls of mud and branches. There was just one big room above an open space downstairs where Roufou slept when he came in from the pasture. Below this was a further space enclosed by planks where the sheep slept with Strenou and the pig which Variou had named Grounniou. And along the walls were the *dolia* full of *kikeri* and barley with the greased *aoula*[1] for the evening's polenta. They slept on fallen leaves: Variou had some matting which he had brought back one feast day from the *makellou*[2] in Noursia. Outside, near the door, was a large stone drinking trough, hollowed out of a single block; grandfather Couprou did not remember ever seeing it anywhere else. As for chairs and a table—there were none. But Variou had brought from the woods some old roughly hewn blocks which they sat on to eat.

In just one corner of the house, on a tree trunk placed upright, a lamp remained lit day and night. It was never short of oil, for Mannia added some every day, pouring it carefully because it was very costly.

"Are you tired, poor pretty little thing—do you want to get in with me? There's just enough room for a man and a little bird like you. You do? Wait, wait a moment and

---

1 Dolia: casks; kikeri: chickpeas; aoula cooking pot. (These are popular or vernacular forms of Latin.)
2 Market.

I'll stop my horse. There, there, whoa, whoa. Come on, jump on the wheel, hold on and I'll grab you. Ah, there we are. Gee-up, horsey, let's go. What's your name, *mel meo*[1]? Poupoula? Ha, that's a pretty name. How tired you look *vitoulou meou*[2]! All alone like that, out on the road? Ha, I see: you don't want to tell me. And where have you come from like that? From near Noursia? And on foot? Well, you must be jolly tired! I'm going to . . . if you like, you can come with me. Don't be afraid, I'm not a bad man. And you might come across lots of bad men on the roads.

"How wet you are, poor little thing, how wet! I could swear you'd come out of the Nar. But tell me now, where exactly are you from? Is it really close to Noursia?

"Tell me, little Poupa, I think you must be the granddaughter of old Couprou. You see, I know him well, your grandfather; we were in the war together once, we two; we were in places with saltwater lakes where the grape seeds were as big as hazelnuts. Yes, we've seen the country. And I can tell you, it was hard marching beneath the sun with tent pegs on our backs. Your grandfather, Poupa, was pouring with sweat. And, you know, we were hungry over there. We had a good *acrocoliou*[3] . . ."

---

1 Honey, sweetie.
2 My little one.
3 Leg of pork, ham.

Strenou had been hunting all day long. Often he left in the morning with Roufou and didn't come home until the evening. When he came back late he scratched at the door, whining, in front of the house. Then Variou got up, grumbling, to let him in. That day, Strenou had enjoyed running after magpies and crows. He had chased a magpie from tree to tree, far into the countryside. Strenou kept running, the magpie hopping in front of him, teasing him. Strenou kept running, even though the heat was oppressive, his tongue hanging out painfully. But he wanted to catch that magpie. "It'll get tired," he said to himself. Strenou kept running.

The wind had got up and was ruffling his coat. In the distance, the magpie was preening its feathers. "Bah," said Strenou to himself, "I'll get it all the same." The hot moist wind was stirring the leaves. The magpie perched in a tree. Strenou sat down to watch it. But then—Strenou had fleas. He turned round for a scratch and—plop! The magpie had disappeared. And Strenou couldn't believe it; he sat there still, watching and watching.

But evening was coming on, with its long shadows and cool wind—the leaves on the trees quivered and night came out of the hedges like a fog. And the tall grasses rippled under the night's breath—falling leaves swirled, and Strenou chased them. He barked, wagging his tail, with the falling leaves dancing around him. Now the birds were chirping in the trees and the wind was blowing up a storm. Then Strenou, sensing the storm, ran off with his tail between his legs. He ran across brambles and thorns, and dead branches crackled under his feet. And a blast of moist wind brought the rain.

The sky was black, covered with clouds, and great masses of shadow stretched out where the hedges and clumps of trees had been. The rain pelted down into the pools and Strenou's fur stuck to his back. The wind moaned and wailed between the trunks of trees and the branches creaked dully.

Then Strenou began to howl at the sky. His lugubrious barking echoed round and round amidst the sound of rain on the leaves. And Strenou ran, howling, whilst the thunder rumbled behind him, deep in the sky. He was soaked from the downpour and his paws were bleeding from the pebbles. He trotted along painfully, whining as he stumbled over the stones . . .

The vicou Touscou[1] was bathed in sunshine. Chimneys threw shadows on the flat roofs; in front of the window nettings flies buzzed in the silence of the sleepy town. The overheated air quivered; the dogs roaming the streets moved with heavy paws. And suddenly the door of the schoolroom opened—class was over—the master was ready for his siesta.

On the roadway of vicou Touscou, around the Temple of Romulus, beneath the Forum's wooden galleries, a noisy crowd was approaching. The sun

---

1 A street or quarter in the Forum, as is vicou Djanou (Janus) below.

beat down directly onto the shaven heads. The children quickly hid their slates under the folds of their tunics, and rushed under the galleries—everything was closed—the stalls of the *argentarii*[1], which so recently had been shining with pieces of gold and silver—were empty; the itinerant jewellers had left the galleries. And in the huge empty marketplace the mosquitoes and big blue flies buzzed around the prostrate dogs.

Over there, the children said to each other, in the vicou Djanou, there must be some shade. They passed close to the Temple of Castor and along the Palace of Djoulia; through the wire netting they could see the rich hangings which kept out the unbearable heat of the sun. The vicou Djanou ran along the shade of the Capitol, dark and empty.

The children were already forming into circles— they were dancing and singing. And whilst some others were having fun lifting and dropping the door knockers to waken the sleepers, a large turbaned eunuch came downstairs to chase them away. He approached, hampered by his long robe. "Will you clear off! Little thieves, sewer rats, crow's dinners! What do you think you're doing, treating people like that! I hope Jupiter carries you off, disturbing honest people!" But the children were already hanging onto his robe, shouting "Gynepatrono! Gynepatrono!"[2] And they struck up the well-known chorus "Plane mago. Valde spado."[3] The eunuch ran back into the house and closed the

---

1 Money changers, bankers.
2 Women's keeper.
3 Total sorcerer; a eunuch certainly.

door. Then they played *par impar*[1]. They put their fists in front of their faces shouting, "quot! quot!"[2] And then they argued, yelling that the others were cheating, that they had opened four fingers not three. Soon there was a general dispute—they were almost coming to blows—but then a little chap with a crafty look proposed playing the game about the will of Marcou Grounniou Corocotta, the little pig—and they agreed.

Then one of them stepped onto a doorstep and started speaking in a nasal whine: "Magirou the cook said to the little pig: 'Come here, you demolisher of houses, you destroyer of the ground, you naughty runaway, today you're going to die.'

"Corocotta, the little pig, said: 'Even if I've done something wrong, if I've committed a crime, if I've broken crockery, please master cook, allow me to live I beg you.' Magirou the cook said, 'Slave, come here: get me my knife from the kitchen so I can spill the blood of this little pig.' And then all the kitchen boys grabbed hold of the little pig—and when Marcou Grounniou Corocotta saw that his end was near, he asked the cook to give him an hour to make his will. He summoned his parents and said to them: 'To my father, big Verrat, I leave thirty bushels of acorns; to my mother, old Truie,[3] I leave forty bushels of flour, and to my sister Quirina I leave thirty bushels of barley. And my body I leave . . .'"

---

1 Odds and evens.
2 "How many?"
3 Sow.

Then the children all started shouting at once. On one side were shouts of "I leave my bristles to the cobblers, my ears to the deaf, my tongue to the lawyers" and on the other side, "I leave my muscles to the weaklings, my feet to the runners, my stomach to the bagpipers." It was a great hubbub, with each one trying to get his word in. And as they were enjoying themselves, they started over again, whilst others marched along arm in arm, chatting about the teacher and the day's lessons. Fanniou had been hit three times on the fingers with the wooden stick for having recited the alphabet badly; the master had even told him, "Wait, wait! Try starting again . . ."

And never a moment free! They'd only got out today because the master was sleepy—and because they'd opened the door quietly. But in the morning they'd have to come to the palestra[1]—then come back with the master and spend the day with him until evening.

It had been a good evening. They were on their way back, happy and satisfied. And Djounia offered her arm to Roudia, snuggling up to her. Their lodging was rather a long way, behind the Via Sacra, in a labyrinth of small muddy streets. But the apartment was so lovely! Up on the sixth floor, beneath the roof, with round windows that were too small for wire mesh looking out

1 A public place for training or exercise in wrestling or athletics.

over the blue countryside. In the mornings the yellow Tiber looked like a gold ribbon in the sparkling sunshine. The thatch which hung from the roof in front of the windows swayed in the fresh morning breeze—swallows often built their nests there. This was where the two "sisters" lived. Djounia's father was an actor at the Circus. The girl had been into men from the age of eleven. She used to tumble around the staircase with the boys, getting caught in dark corners. The father had sold her twice, but as she was becoming more independent he'd had enough and thrown her out.

For two months she lived on the street; at night she would take late passers-by under the arcades of closed houses—avoiding any telltales in the streets and passageways—sleeping in the outskirts, in a shed, on straw, amongst the pickaxes and rakes. She passed her days stretched out on the grass, by the side of the river, in the sunshine. She loved the smell of fresh grass—the oblivion of thinking about nothing, sleeping a sweet sleep, woken occasionally by a little creature running over her face. And then one evening, as she returned to the city, she met Roudia at the corner of one of the forum's galleries. She liked the look of her straightaway. Roudia was very taken by the thought of such a depraved union. She would be the man and Djounia the woman. Roudia had money. Djounia gave her presents. She adored her. She gave her everything—her jewellery, her beautiful new clothes—and she kissed her enthusiastically. As soon as she went outside she trembled. There were so many telltales in the streets! And gradually she felt a great hatred of men growing inside her. What she had done for pleasure at the beginning now seemed to her an unbearable burden. Her only love was her darling Roudia. It was for her that she earned the money—to buy her dresses, to offer her necklaces, rings, bracelets.

Roudia was a brunette, Djounia blonde and slim. Roudia was not nasty, but she could be curt. Sometimes she made dreadful scenes, tearing clothes, damaging furniture, smashing crockery. But she had a good heart, giving away all she owned, unable to see a beggar at her door without throwing him a handful of coins—tears in her eyes when hearing of injustice or cruelty. Her anger could boil up—she would often beat Djounia during the fits of madness which took hold of her sometimes. And then it was a torrent of abuse: "You dog's spawn, *loupia defoutouta*[1], you old bitch—your mother's curses be on you."

"Shush, Poupoula, shush! You mustn't talk like that. The Lord[2] forbids it. Do you know how we live? A thousand times, we're a thousand times more miserable than you! Look at Rahel here and Abimelek. Do you think they have work? Ah, you see, the Lord has abandoned us. A curse on Rome and their Goyim[3]. But we too, we know how to put a curse on them; we know herbs, we can kill them with our spells, those spawn

---

1 Worn-out prostitute.
2 "El" in the original text (Yaweh).
3 Goyim: non-Jews.

of dogs, may the Lord damn them. But, Rahel and Abimelek, the Lord has abandoned us. He's on the side of the rebels, with the Goyim and their damned Jesus. They say Jesus died out there in Canaan. In truth, he was too learned for a rabbi; you see my children, he did nothing but harm. We're no longer together. Like in the old days, we Jews—that's why it's not working. Ah, may the Lord confound them, those who adore Jesus. They're with the Romans, against us—oh misery, misery! Are we still what we were before? Do our men still have the Megillah? Since the damned Goyim came we're miserable and hounded. Before, the Romans left us in peace. But since Rabbi Jesus (may the Lord curse him—and yet he knew the scriptures)—since that dog's spawn appeared the Romans have pursued and hunted us like animals—and yet we were peaceful; it was them, the Goyim who rose up! And now the Romans say we drink the blood of children on the first day of Passover, with the first piece of matzo and that we adore that unclean animal, the pig, because Moses forbade us to eat it! And yet, Rahel, Abimelek, we adore only the Lord—you know the song from the Megillah:

> "*Schema Israel! Adonaï elohaïnou, Adonaï ekhot*
> "*Ah, woe betide them! Woe! May Yahweh confound them.*
> "*May the Lord forgive me for having named him—I did not invoke him in vain. Woe to the Goyim and the Romans, woe!*"

❋

That evening, beneath the Sublicius Bridge, there were great festivities. The beggars in their rags, the thieves saying nothing, the brutal stranglers, all threw themselves into the orgy. Below the arches they danced wildly round in circles, prostitutes on the arms of thieves, intertwined, in step with each other. The bonfires of vine shoots, crackling as they burned, showered the separate groups with sudden flashes of light; the fire threw up forked tongues of flame along the pillars, clinging to the blocks of stone. In a corner, squatting on a heap of pebbles, a beggar was silently sipping from his bowl. His twisted legs were covered in bandages down to the ankles; ragged pieces of his cloak hung between his knees; with his head in his hands, he mused. The red skin swelled, pinched, between his gnarled fingers and clumps of the white hairs of his beard poked through. He was thinking about the old days of his youth—when the prostitutes, alarmed by the summer evening breezes, had clung to his clothes at street corners—where he lived with his *souccouve*[1] in the Soubourre[2]. He thought about all those young girls he had trained in that Soubourre, in the women's quarters that his darling Loukia had so capably managed—in that Soubourre where the silent houses came alive during the siesta and when night fell—when masked men mingled with the shadows, leaning against the walls. There, behind the

---

1 Concubine.
2 Part of Rome renowned for its low life.

wire mesh of the windows, in the shade of the Persian carpets and the wall hangings from Asia Minor, how many hours had passed in sensual pleasures! And later those girls had seduced emperors—and it was he, poor humble Virgou, who had shown them how—he and Loukia.

But the informers had closed his house and taken Loukia far, far away. Virgou didn't know exactly where, but to some forbidding underground chamber, darker than the Latomies[1], where on the orders of the Lords she had to concoct potions to stimulate their numbed senses, accompanying the hissing of the boiling concoctions with her slow monotonous incantations.

No doubt she was keeping watch by the fire, her loose hair floating above her naked shoulders, still waving her wand over the boiling mixture.

But he, Virgou, had worn himself out with all those young girls; he had fallen into poverty and then into destitution; and now he was a beggar. His tainted blood gave him hideous ulcers on his legs and leprosy was beginning to make his scalp swell.

And far away his Loukia had forgotten him, amongst her boxes of incense smelling of *achante*, her azure *aerizoulae* in her ears, the fragrances of *aglaophois* and *ivraie* all around, whilst the *alloukitae*[2] swarmed round her smoking lamp.

---

1 Stone quarry caves.
2 *Achante:* strong smelling matter; *Aerisoulae:* turquoises; *Aglaophotis:* an herb used for spells; *Alloukitae:* midges.

As the curtains of Syrian cloth shimmered, their heavy folds weighing on the embroidered cushions, she rolled about gently. The light of the silver lamps shone from the ceiling, and circles of light illuminated the rugs and floated along the hangings. She undid her *zonoule*[1] from its tight hold around her hips and the white flesh of her breasts showed through the rolls of her tunic which now lay along her thighs. And against the dark colours of the rug where she stretched out, her white body showed up wonderfully.

Ah, how handsome he had been! And now where was he? Gone, gone. The dark waters of the yellow Tiber surged beneath the Sublicius Bridge; the lanterns of the moored boats pierced the darkness with points of light. All was dead in the great city; all was dead in Poupa's heart. How black the water was beneath the bridge. How enticing it was, with its ripples and its eddies and its sinister whirlpools. One plunge—it would all be over—Variou—Mannia—gone with the loved one. Nothing left! Nothing left!

But then sharp teeth seized the robe as it fell; a joyful barking echoed around the arches: Strenou was there; Strenou had saved his mistress. How he trembled with joy! How he pawed her!

How he licked Poupa's face. And Poupa closed her eyes; for she was seized with the horror of death.

---

1 Belt.

They danced below the statues interspersed with grinning fawns. In the distance the dull white of the marbles lightened the darkness, behind the flaming torches. And beneath the portico of the temple, along the urns set up on the wide old parapet to receive alms, there were muffled sniggers and sounds of tickling. In the madness of the dance white robes fluttered, in and out of sight, coming and going; breath came in gasps, bosoms heaved—and it was so good. Warm air rose from the sleeping town towards the hills; a humming, suffocating atmosphere.

At that time of night the prostitutes had all gone home—they would be comfortably sleeping, or sobbing in some hovel. But up here, the ladies were enjoying themselves. The eunuchs were waiting, sitting on the floor or squatting, with legs crossed, tormenting their mules with the points of their silver-knobbed sticks. Their saffron robes stood out against the grey paving slabs, giving off an odour of cinnamon. With their heads bowed towards their knees they dreamed of the heat of Syria or the silver mines of Hibernia.

How far they had come! At the age of fifteen they had still been roaming the snow-covered mountains, with the goats. They drank milk—they lived in the fresh air, with the pure sunshine and the blue sky. There the sun's rays beamed straight down on your head. You stretched out in the shade of an ancient rock and, with the muzzle of your good old dog between your knees you looked into his eyes, dreaming, for a long time. And he licked your hands, gave you his faithful look and dreamed with you.

And in the evening as the shadows lengthened you came down the little path with the goats; the bats flew out of the bushes and the birds, awakened, chirped. You could hear the sound in the grass of a snake sliding back to his hole; the cricket sang in the last golden flames of the dying day; the rocks were taking on a grey tinge and the first shiver of night made the leaves tremble in the trees. A cool wind made your cloak billow and ruffled the goats' coats; the dog sniffed the perfumed breeze, his nose in the air, and the yellow-headed broom trees undulated like the ocean waves.

Lower down the rabbits took refuge in the undergrowth and shadows gathered around the old oaks, already giving the mountain a sinister appearance. But soon you were at the cottage, your mother at the door with a spoon in her hand, your father coming up from the fields, tired out, with his pickaxe over his shoulder.

Lord in heaven, where is it now, that Spanish scrubland—and your fathers' cottages and the friendly herds. Everything—the Romans destroyed everything. Those hard Italian men came, with their shaven heads and their mocking laughter. They had burned the houses and eaten the herds. Your father had died of exhaustion along the way and your mother starved to death in the mountain's undergrowth. She hadn't wanted to go with the soldiers—she had run away, shouting hoarsely like a wild animal, dishevelled, ferocious—throwing stones at those who came near her.

The young men had been taken away, pell-mell. They had curly hair and soft slightly brown skin. They were looked after, well fed. They were taken into the mountains near Osca. The soldiers came down along the Cinca and crossed the plain of Sourdao, taking them to Ilerda, where they'd come from. And then from there, without a break, merchants had taken them to Tarraco, across the black mountains of Iakketa and Ilercao. Then there were some tough stages of the journey to reach the sea. The mountains were dry and barren—from the dry salty wind—and the sun beat down mercilessly. On arrival at Tarraco they had been subjected to the shameful mutilation, but without pain. They had been made to sleep, by drinking an infusion of poppy seeds. And those who were fully grown had become gigolos to pleasure the Roman ladies.

They had been put on board ship, piled in like cattle. Many remained along the Italian coasts, at Popoulonia, at Cosa or at Alsion—the others had disembarked at Ostia. And came to Rome, to a merchant's. Soon the ladies of Rome were buying them. They were so pretty with their white teeth and their dark eyes. And they spoke Latin with a slight guttural accent which the ladies found charming. Now, they were hollow, used up. Their long robes floated around them; they croaked like girls with their hoarse voices, dazed, drained. Sometimes a shaft of sunlight would enter their heads. And then they thought about the old mountain with its broom, and the house so far away, so far. Instead of living a strong life, like men, like mountain dwellers, in their barren homeland, amongst the dry undergrowth of the black mountain, they wilted in the shade of wall hangings, the softness of cushions, like wildflowers torn from the ground.

Suddenly came the sound of tambourines, the bells tinkled. The dance was starting up again. The women laughed, pushing, hugging and touching each other. Couples disappeared behind the pillars. The warm air no longer rose from below. The cool morning breeze was already ruffling the light clothing. And after the night of sensuous dances the women had themselves carried away in their litters.

All returned to silence. The night watchman came to give his three cries in the square—the dogs barked—and near the dark buildings, shadows slid furtively along the walls. The emperor's police were at work; the informers were in action—and in the distance the dull rhythmic steps of the imperial patrolmen echoed on the great pavements.

Torches preceded them. When they arrived at the square the captain ordered: "Sta!" and about turn. Those carrying the torches illuminated the walls. The temple guard came out. Nothing had been happening that evening.

Then the patrol resumed its march. Darkness reigned once more. In the distance was the sound of the dull rhythmic footsteps—the soldiers were leaving. And amid the silence a cock crowed in the countryside.

Along the dusty road, the shady paths, Poupa was still running, with Strenou following, her robe tucked between her legs so that she could jump over the hedges. In the green meadows the flies circled madly over the ponds and the frogs croaked in the silence of the countryside. How good it felt to run! Strenou thought so too; he wagged his tail and licked his lips. But Strenou was crafty. He would probably snatch a corncrake in some hedge, running through it whilst Poupa continued forwards. She looked nice with her straw hat pushed back and her rustic scarf over her shoulders! And she certainly appealed to Roufou.

He watched for her through the branches when she was due to arrive; he whittled elder wood into whistles for her.

Often he brought chickpeas which he stole from Variou's barn. On those days they would dig a hole with their hands and fill it with small branches and dead leaves. They would light a small fire and then, sitting gravely face to face, would roast their chickpeas on the pointed end of a stick—or they would play king and queen. Then they made a throne out of flat stones, in the shade somewhere. The queen would sit there and the king would leave to guard the sheep. Often the queen, after playing with the straw hat, would fall asleep on her throne. Then, when the king returned, he would make her a pillow out of moss and lay her gently onto it . . .

The Gold Hatpin

FOR the past few moments the glass-panelled door, opening and closing in the building's bay frontage, had no longer drawn the attention of the women. The Englishmen, coming in, going out, with their felt hats, their wide trousers, their short pipes in their mouths, attracted no interest. The little cyclist with the innocent air remained alone in a corner, left alone by the elderly minders. They were all watching a dark-haired, pale-faced man who had sat down at a table at the back. He had extraordinarily thick eyebrows, so bushy that they met across the top of his nose; pinched nostrils, and a very red mouth; around his neck was a large golden collar like a dog's, flecked with diamonds; two yellow gold bracelets with a single opal in the middle encircled his long red gloves. His upper body was crammed into a corset; but the loose material of his trousers revealed the trembling of his thin legs. Most of all, he had strange eyes, clear and grey but bottomless, lit by a cold look as though through a tarnished mirror.

"There's your little sweetie," cried Nini-Powder-Face to Velvet-Choker, "I want to borrow him." Julie-Sweet-

Voice, passing close by the man, brushed his neck with her bosom, scarcely covered by its white net fabric, as she hummed: "They're not droopy rogues, they're scallywags—they're blushing!" Young Five-Minutes-in-my-Bed, the former queen of the little tarts of Place Maubert, who was now the princess of the boulevard's tittle-tattle, came and looked up into his face and burst out laughing.

The man did not move. Then Velvet-Choker slowly stood up and came to sit opposite him. Her skin was so white that her neck seemed to have a dark line around it from the shadow of her high collar. Her black hair was like a heavy helmet beneath her Directoire-fashion hat. Gently and clearly she said to the man: "How are you, dear? It's a long time since I've seen you."

She had never met him. But she was crafty enough to know that obsessives can be taken in by an appearance of familiarity. The man with the dog's collar had an obsession, to be sure. You couldn't see it from the empty look he turned towards her, from the mark of indifference and apathy which clouded his pupils. His legs looked dead beneath the table. "Easy pickings," thought Velvet-Choker. "He's good for twenty gold pieces I reckon." And she began to think it over as she sipped her punch. A foot fetishist? . . . nah . . . he hadn't even looked at her feet. Bondage . . . he would have picked a woman with a hard look. Maybe the choker . . . Unconsciously she picked at her fingers with the pin of her gold filigree brooch.

Suddenly the man's eyes reddened. Blood spots appeared at the edges of his lower eyelids. His pupils glowed with shining life. His face creased, the glum expression gone. He stamped his feet. He paid the waiter and, quickly putting on his overcoat, led Velvet-Choker out. "Good night," Nini-Powder-Face wished her, "Madame is off to bed." Velvet-Choker turned and saw Julie-Sweet-Voice laughing with Five-Minutes-in-my-Bed. The tongue-waggers accused poor Choker of acting out all the passions without feeling any. But the man with the bracelets seemed not to have heard anything. He walked jerkily. Sometimes his knees seemed to give way. When he spoke it was with a drawl, the words disjointed. He asked Velvet-Choker to come home with him.

She agreed, after a moment's hesitation. She would certainly not stay until the morning. The man with the bracelets was tired out; once the passion was spent he would sleep the sleep of the dead. They went along the boulevards. At the corner of the boulevard Saint-Martin the man, who had fallen back into his apathetic state, his legs moving mechanically, straightened up with a jolt when he was confronted by the blade of old Pa-the-Knife. The old man was rapidly chopping up his cake with the sharp blade, shoving the crumbs into his basket. The street urchins were coming up with their little hands outstretched, asking for "just a penn'orth of crumbs, Mister Pa-the-Knife." Then, grubbing around in the cake crumbs they often came across a silver coin, swept in there accidentally. "Done you for tenpence, old Pa-the-Knife," yelled the little brats as they skedaddled. But old Pa-the-Knife carried on slicing, unmoved. The man with the bracelets watched the blade falling, and trembled so violently that it gave Velvet-Choker quite a turn. The night was lightening over the rooftops as the gas lamps were extinguished.

Then the man turned left, into a side street, opened a door with his key. To the far side of the staircase a bluish light shone from the windows opening onto the narrow well of a courtyard. The apartment had wall hangings. The double doors closed silently. Light from the lamps revealed a bedroom with a large mirror at the far end. There was a low bed. Near the bed were shelves holding an opium pipe and milky white bottles full of a greenish paste. A pale pot, half full of a black jelly, held five or six long yellow hatpins. Opposite the mirror, to the left of the door, two green wall hangings closed off an oblong alcove almost as high as the ceiling. There were three mirrors over the bed.

At a glance Velvet-Choker realised she had not been wrong. But she didn't see any bundles of birch canes, nor pincers for nails, nor cats o' nine tails. Nothing but green and gold bottles, melted green paste, narrow pipes with silver bowls, and the yellow hatpins. A stale odour seemed to be given off by the walls and furniture. It lingered heavily in the air and clung to clothes. "It must be one of those pastes," thought Velvet-Choker. There was the dull sound of drips falling.

Standing in front of the mirror she started unfastening her silk bodice. She let down the heavy tresses of her hair, then put them up fixing them here and there with hairpins; to check they were in the right places, she bent towards the mirror. Suddenly she saw the man carefully lifting the green curtain of the alcove; seeing her move, he quickly let go and moved away.

Then Velvet-Choker saw in the mirror a pale jagged smudge against the curtain material. She looked more closely; it was a hand, waxy yellow, the fingers clenched, sticking out between the curtains. Velvet-Choker cried out, "My God!" and ran towards the alcove. The man threw himself in front of her; she pushed him aside and snatched away the material. She fell in a dead faint on the floor at what she saw.

The niche had six shelves. And on five of them were stretched women's bodies, dirty yellow, with brown and purple bruising. They were totally naked, with earrings in their ears and bracelets on their arms. The head and hand of the body at the top were overhanging, and from its mouth ran a dribble of blood; the drops splashed regularly onto the floor. But their faces looked peaceful, even smiling with a sort of calm joy.

Coming to straight away, Velvet-Choker rushed to the door in her underwear, her hair hanging loose. "Five women! Five women!" she cried. "The monster! Police commissioner! My God! Police! Where's the door? To come with such a man . . . Help! . . . Murderer!" She stood open-mouthed, eyes wide, in front of the man who seemed to have changed completely.

His pale face was pink now; his eyes shone with an internal fire. In his hand he held one of the long yellow hatpins. With one bound he was at the side of Velvet-Choker with his hand over her mouth. And with his lips to her ear he whispered urgently to her:

"Yes, my love, I killed them. But they died without realising it. They were struck once and my ecstasy came as they passed out on the spot. You, my darling, will be aware of it all. With your pale flesh, your large gentle eyes, your black wavy hair, you will be able to die slowly, because you'll know that you're dying. You will fall gradually back, you'll feel the blood running from your veins, the darkness will rise slowly from your bosom to wrap itself around you. Those women there had no love, they'd given it all away. When I looked at you I saw that you feel nothing. I saw it when you were pricking your fingers with the pin of your brooch—ah!—when you were calculating your price. I saw it when you came in here and you were looking for the instruments of torture. If nothing can make you feel anything, what's the point of living? Me, I only live for each shudder of pleasure. Be quiet! Oh! Be quiet. Don't struggle. They died in an instant, it was supreme rapture for me—as I sank this gold hatpin into their necks. You, you'll pass out and you'll die drop by drop; you'll feel pleasure as great as mine—as I slowly force this sharp golden tip through your neck."

At these words a burning feeling passed through Velvet-Choker, already half-conscious. A ball of fire mounted from the pit of her stomach into the back of her throat. Her horror turned into a furious desire; her pupils were fixed beneath the bottomless gaze holding them. And she simply uttered a deep sigh when the man with the bracelets, fooling her too, thrust the gold hatpin into the back of her neck. A small red stain marked her white neck where the shadow of her high collar had so often placed a velvet choker.

The Psychology of the
Three-card Trick

BEHIND the Caulaincourt bridge stretches waste
ground bordered by hovels; the town is desolate
there, the houses falling apart and hastily plastered;
sometimes a potholed road cuts through the shacks;
the inns are huts made of branches patched with dried
earth; there are taverns with windows on three sides
with punched-in panes all over them, covered with
paper strips. The counter is empty, the Griffe law[1]
displayed on the bare wall. The bottles are out back.
When you go in, "mine host" emerges with a revolver
in his "paw"; he pours with one hand, with the other
he aims his "shooter" to encourage payment. Drinkers
prowl around, serving themselves on the benches by
the light of a candle; the only sound is of the rain
pounding against the window panes, the wind shifting
the wooden slats and sometimes a paper pane tearing
apart.

---

1 La loi Griffe of 1889 laid down the legal requirements for wine
making.

In winter the three-card tricksters emigrate there. They abandon their suits and silk hats; they wear knitted clothes and caps. Life is too expensive in Paris without the races; for it to take off successfully you need bright sunshine, lines of Englishmen with their round caps and their tailored jackets, carriages full of fearful faces—and a good non-stopping train to Chantilly. But when the city lights up, in November, December, the three-card trick leaves; it gets played here and there, apprehensively, at a street corner on a Saturday with a bit of sales patter. When the north wind gets sharp the folk don't stop; the three cards fly away; the trickster packs up his cards, whistles a tune, picks up a "fag end" and lights it. Then he goes back up the Butte Montmartre, off to the countryside too—but in winter—he is "broke" so he goes back "downtown" to the Boulevard Rochechouart. At night he sleeps on planks somewhere. By day he "knocks off" for a while at one moment, at another he "grafts" a little, if that doesn't give him too much of a shock; in the evening he goes to guzzle his "hot toddy" at the tavern with the windows where the publican holds his shooter in his paw.

The man I saw one day in this deserted location, at the Zifolo, was hard, thin, red-faced. The Zifolo stretches across the front of the tavern like a rain-rusted tin Mirliton[1] creaking in the wind. The room has that worrying look of halls with high windows where light

1 It is possible that Schwob is referring to Le Mirliton, a tavern founded by Aristide Bruant in 1885 at 84 Boulevard Rochechouart.

comes in on all sides as if you were being watched simultaneously through all the panes of glass. But the man did not seem in the least anxious. He felt at ease, amongst his comrades. It was clear from his relaxed elbows, the casualness of his cap. He had a clear gaze but his eyes were the colour of absinthe, the dangerous eyes of an evildoer in which his intelligence is masked. He slid three cards onto the table with captivating speed: "Spades lose, clubs lose, hearts win!—Watch the heart, it's smart! Who wants clubs, that's for nubs! Who's taking spades, that's for maids! Hearts win— spades lose—clubs lose—tick, it's gone—hearts win, it's a spin—spades lose—clubs lose—and here come the cops!" His voice was a hoarse, muted drawl, with emphasis on some syllables, resonances in places, whilst his expression remained impenetrable. For this man realised the power of the eyes for the player, and his were of a bottomless green.

But as the sales patter was having no effect, he gradually became silent, and, having a drink with me, he began a conversation.

"We're no longer in the time of Fiferlin," he said. "He was the king of the three-card trick. Things really livened up with him around. He would get onto a nonstopping train; no way of getting off. The punters were in the carriage. The team was there, the hustler and his accomplices; the hustler got the cards out; finally it worked. It's annoying, not being able to get off; the people were fed up, so in the end, they went along with the game.

"It was Fiferlin who gave the 'bonnet'[1] game its name, 'lingerie'. A great name, eh? So we hustlers are the 'linges', we hold the bonnets. Of course, deep down it's all mickey-taking, all lies. But you, if you're the 'baron'[2], I'm the marquis, aren't I? So, if I'm the hustler, let's suppose, I'm the baron, I do a trick, a good one; but you, you're the other baron, why would you try to see the card?

"That's how it works with the lingerie. You want to see the card, okay? Well, it's not the real one. You'll see it, but it's not the one. The accomplices have to understand how it works. Suppose the card is on the left—I say 'tick'; if it's in the middle I say 'spin'; if I put it under my right hand, I say 'here come the cops'. That's another of Fiferlin's inventions.

"If the targets were not thieves there'd be no three-card trick. You're all the same, you all want to cheat. If you were honest, you'd put your finger randomly on one of the three cards. But the target, what does he do? He peeks underneath, has a squint. Once he thinks he's got the card, I do a sleight of hand. Where is it now? The gentleman who just cheated says: 'It's the middle one'—ha! Not true, it's jumped to the left.

"Then the target says to himself: 'I've been conned; I need to keep an eye out.' So I turn down the corner of the card—nothing much—the card's quite crinkled anyway. The dupe, wanting to pull a fast one, laughs and thinks: 'He's not up to much, this trickster; his card is turned down—I'll get this one.' Yes, but as I

---

1 Three-card trick.
2 Accomplice.

deal I straighten the corner and I mark the other, the losing one. Then, who's in the soup! The thief!

"Secretly marking the card is the most difficult bit. You need to really know your 'bonnet' and have nimble fingers. I pick a punter who looks sure of himself, who doesn't want to know. But I've seen he still has a thousand franc note in his pocket. I need to get my hands on it. I've got my team; it won't work without them. My accomplice identifies the target, sweet-talks him along these lines more or less: 'Monsieur, you've lost a lot of money; I've been seriously done over too. These people are crooks—but I've got them. I've just marked the card with a circle of cigar ash; the trickster didn't see anything, we can bet on it and get our money back.' The target takes the bait—because basically he's a thief. He arrives, looks at the marked card. I play the idiot. But I've dipped my little finger in the cigar ash; I wipe it from the good card, and put the mark onto the bad one. I'm not the one who's stealing—it's the other who's in deep water."

The man became gradually more animated with these explanations. He seemed convinced. He had a deep contempt for mankind; he only knew it through the card trick. The real thief in this game was not the wretched conjuror who makes the cards jump around, not the scared starveling who picks up the cards with a shout of "Here come the cops"—it was the rich gentleman, the middle-class racegoer, the high-ranking person, the punter; the three-card trick was a protest. You steal from me, so I steal. All gamers are thieves; let's be more of a thief than him. That's only fair.

"And now in winter what do you do?" I asked him.

"Oh, in winter we're broke. I do a bit of stealing now and again—I work for the black gang." He showed a sort of pride, boasting about stealing: there was no sign in his impenetrable glance of worry about admitting to it. He was a loudmouth but I'd got his measure. Just now, we'd been the thieves. The roles had changed. I gently pointed this out to the man. He shrugged his shoulders; the clarity of his gaze wavered for a moment; then he abruptly moved away.

I went to the races the other day. Just as the train was leaving three men jumped into the carriage. Five minutes later the three cards appeared on a cloth, coming from I don't know where. "Spades lose—clubs lose—hearts win. Watch the heart—it's smart. Who wants clubs—that's for nubs." Gradually I got interested in the flying card, I bet a gold coin. And as I instinctively watched the bottom of the ace of hearts which passed back and forth, the dealer gave me an ironical look. I recognised the man from the Zifolo, and I blushed crimson. The man had won the game. I had not been able to resist the psychology of honest men; I *was stealing*.

The Tiber's Nuptials

A slanting sunbeam showed him the way
(Catulle Mendès[1], *Hesperus*)

NEAR HORTA[2], the Nar flows into the Tiber, with no bar, in fact with no waves, no foam; a long yellow just slightly choppy line marks the merger of the two rivers. Reeds grow on the Nar's banks, mixed with gorse where the kingfishers and wild ducks come; willows dip their weeping leaves and their slanting branches into the dying river. The current, unable to continue, calms its waters, now peaceful and covered with lilies opening and closing their large white petals over their yellow stamens; the fat water beetles with their shiny wing cases paddle beneath the water between the stems of red grass; the sticklebacks raise their sharp fins below the leaves.

The goddess Naria was washed willingly up to the bank, amongst the reeds which curved away gently

---

1 A French writer and poet, 1841-1909.
2 Orte in modern Italian.

and moved apart as they brushed against her body. She stretched out on the grass, her streaming hair strewn over her back, her chin propped up on her hands, her elbows on the turf. The shining drops covered her body with pink, green and azure pearls; her black eyes shone deeply, like inky diamonds, as they ranged over the yellow line separating the waters of the Nar from the billows of the Tiber; she always stopped at this place; her white limbs had never been soiled by the muddy eddies surging in the distance; the Nar's ripples murmured "Adieu" as they passed through the reeds close to her.

Tiber, the god with the golden beard, had for a long time been in love with the goddess Naria. But the nymph whom fate had brought to him would not yield, and the god was becoming pale with anger. He made his river boil as it flowed; its angry waves stirred up the pebbles, the earth and the sand, crashing along with the dead wood and rotten leaves. The muddy waters swelled and flooded the banks, covering the meadows with a black slime which smothered the grass and flowers. Lumps of filth were forced back into the drains of Rome and overflowed into the streets, where they rotted in the sun. In the outskirts, the residents moved away from the riverbanks where the building foundations were being eaten away; epidemics of plague spread amongst the people, and the furious populations insulted the gods.

Then the magistrates consulted the *aougouri* and the *harouspikes*[1] who spent a long time studying the sacred

---

1 Auguries and haruspices; the latter were persons who inspected the entrails of sacrificial victims in order to foretell the future.

texts. Deep in the gloomy temples they huddled over lighted coals where shoulders of mutton were roasting and they paid careful attention to the sound of crackling. They snatched bloody livers from the steaming breasts of lambs, examining them with a worried look, as they nodded their heads. Finally they decided that a ceremony was needed to offer expiatory libations to the angry god of the Tiber.

A solemn procession moved along the banks of the river. The priests stopped at the Aemilius Bridge and pronounced the incantations in solemn tones. The crowd listened thoughtfully, their gaze fixed on the threatening waves which did not recede. The chants over, the procession crossed the bridge in silence. The head priest stopped at the far side, calling aloud the name of the god Tiber, Rome's protector. Then into the foaming waves he cast *scriblitae*[1], pastries and honey *plakentae*[2] which two priests behind him were carrying in baskets. Then he took a silver amphora, quickly tipped onto the bridge its stopper of perfumed oil and gently poured the red wine into the river. For a moment the Tiber was tinged with red, near the far pillar of the Sublicius Bridge; the beggars and the ragged children clapped their hands happily, then the procession set off again in total silence, to return to the city.

But the god Tiber was unmoved by the ceremony. He foamed still, stirring up his mud. The yellow line of Horta retreated imperceptibly, back into the Nar,

---

1 Tarts.
2 Sacred cakes.

which was drawing back from the Tiber. The mud smeared the waterlilies, the red grasses, the meadows where Naria had lain, and the willow branches; the water beetles and the sticklebacks were gone and the goddess Naria, stopped in her tracks, watched from her position on the bank as her river dulled over, her eyes full of tears.

However, the god Tiber, nervously ploughing through the waves, watched the weeping goddess from the surface of the water. She spent a long time thinking; as the last rays of the sun were hovering on the horizon she disappeared into the woods. The god Tiber roamed the night with more hope; for amusement he went to find little Farfar, his slave. The small stream, Farfar, was almost empty; he jumped for joy when he saw the god Tiber; he snatched a water lily which was growing on his bank; he picked up a glow-worm and wrapped it between the lily's transparent leaves, and danced along in front of the god Tiber, waving his lantern on its green stem.

"Farfar," said the god Tiber, "this evening I made Naria weep."

"So much the better," replied Farfar, laughing scornfully. "She's so snooty. She sent me away because I was teasing Himella. She's bigger than me, Himella, but that didn't stop us getting on well. We would go around together at night; she let me put my arm round her; I lifted her up and she let herself go in my arms; her kisses were as fresh as the dew I could breathe on the waterlily's flower. The goddess Naria saw us; she frowned. Since then, Himella turns away when I come past; all I get now are furtive glances; but I watch her from a distance and the blue flowers I see hardly bending beneath her toes showed me that she watered them with her salty tears."

As he finished his story there was a slight movement behind a tree to the right. The god Tiber turned his head and saw two gentle eyes shining beneath the leaves. "It's Himella," said Farfar. "How dazzling her eyes are! When we come near, she will run away." But the god Tiber approached: nothing moved under the tree's leaves. Farfar swung his lantern between the branches; a white arm suddenly stretched out and drew the lily into the hiding place; then they heard a stifled ripple of laughter. The hand appeared again and gently touched the god Tiber on the shoulder. "Come, Himella," begged Farfar, "don't be afraid. Look, I'll jump onto a branch of the tree; I won't come down on the ground; I just want to see you."

Like a doe Himella emerged gracefully from the copse and looked around fearfully. Glancing up she smiled at Farfar, sitting on a branch of the oak tree she had just left:

"O god Tiber," said Himella in a clear voice, "my mistress Naria instructed me to bring you to her; we'll find her at Lake Velino, where she's waiting for you."

"I'll follow you," replied the god Tiber. "But come down Farfar and light the way for us. Himella and I will walk behind you."

That was how they walked, slipping quickly through the wood. They flew over the ravines and abysses, without disturbing the night birds, who did not notice their passing. They crossed the mountain and came down to the edge of the Himella. Its steep banks were covered in mist: Himella touched the fog with a finger; it lit up and the three gods disappeared into its luminosity. Farfar continued in front, swinging the waterlily whose twinkling flower made a point of radiance amongst the haze. The god Tiber followed silently, and Himella floated at his side. They descended towards Lake Velino which could already be seen, its dimly lit expanse stretching towards the horizon.

The air vibrated with a piercing harmonious sound, to which Farfar responded quietly; close to the god Tiber a flapping of wings could be heard, and Himella's outstretched hand caressed unseen beings. An intense glow appeared on the lake, where a white conch shell floated, its interior a bluish reflection. The goddess Naria was resting there, leaning on her elbows; her loose hair spread over her dazzling body; Himella rushed towards her and sat at her feet. The god Tiber stood before her, head bowed. Farfar was perched on top of the shell; he was watching Himella below him with desire.

"Will you forgive me, goddess," murmured the god Tiber, "for the tears I made you shed?"

"Alas," said Naria, "I had no choice. When you were pursuing me, I could run away from you. But you have soiled my river; that is why I sent for you."

"O goddess," said the Tiber, "you know I have loved you for years. Don't be angry: why were you avoiding such pleasure?"

"And how could I not avoid it?" replied Naria more sharply. "You spoil everything that comes near you. You fill the clear water of my Nar with mud; you dull the mountain streams, you stagnate in the drains of Rome, the city to which you brought civilisation, to which you introduced through Ostia the foreigners who ruined it. I am free, and happy in my purity."

"O goddess," said the Tiber, "yield to me, yield to me! You can stay for ever in the mountains, since you love them: but I shall come to find you. O Naria, it's not good to live alone. The great gods in heaven don't do that. Look at Louna[1], she wanders, miserably, behind the hunting dogs, the priests on earth howl at night with the pain of their sterility. Follow the example of Mavor et Venous[2]; they're no less powerful and they govern all men."

But Naria shook her head, not responding; her look was lost amongst the drifting mists. Himella had stood up again; her feet were dipped in the lake; her hand rested on the wall of the conch shell, and, not speaking, she exchanged slow glances with Farfar. Naria did not feel the hand of the god Tiber taking her own, the first golden arrow of the sun, no doubt sent by the hand of the god Desire, pierced her heart. She submitted to the embrace of the Tiber, and Himella, trembling, embraced Farfar. The light breath of morning brought upon the water the sounds of the countryside, the bleating of the sheep, the lowing of the bulls, the crowing of the cocks and the cackling of the hens.

---

1 The moon.
2 Mars and Venus.

The mists of the lake lifted beneath the caresses of the sun's beams and, with them, the gods' shapes were fading away. Farfar and Himella had almost disappeared; the god Tiber was melting away and Naria swooned in the haze. When the sun's rays poured their dazzling whiteness over the lake the shapes of the gods had been carried away by the mist.

Thus were celebrated the nuptials of the Tiber and the Nar.

The Assassins

THE gang which M Goron[1] has just nabbed at Asnières is a typical criminal outfit. You'd think we were back in the good old days of the rue du Temple affair which Eugène Sue described in *Les Mystères de Paris*. The widow Berlant today, in boulevard Voltaire, has no reason to envy the fortunate mother of Fifi Vollard, a.k.a. Tortillard[2]. I don't think there has been any progress since then—unless it's that the assassins of the Soufflard gang were grown men, thirty to forty years old, whilst those of the Berlant gang aren't yet twenty. But if public morality has declined it's not in that direction. There is no more criminality today than there was fifty years ago: children, instead of tripping someone up to facilitate a robbery with violence, now wield the knife themselves, that's all.

---

1 Marie-François Goron (1847-1933): French soldier from 1865, and police officer from 1881, eventually head of the Sûreté; he later became a crime writer in retirement.
2 Fifi Vollard was the anti-hero of two *feuilletons* by Constant Guéroult (1814-1882), *Le crime de la rue du Temple* and *La bande à Fifi Vollard*, the first of which deals with a murder and robbery committed by the Soufflard gang.

It is to this persistence in the customs of criminality that I wish to draw attention. The Courbevoie assassins belong to the old tradition in which they were schooled. Doré, who planned the business, was a butcher's apprentice. I hasten to add that there are good and bad butchers. But the bad could not be worse. For over a century the abattoirs have provided a rich harvest for the guillotine. The lower orders amongst butchers supply their share of recruits to the armies of criminals and to the executioner's escorts. Butchers who mix with the dangerous classes have adopted their special language and even adapted it for their own purposes. The last song of Aristide Bruant is the monologue of a "loucherbème[1] bird": this "bird" has so immersed herself in the habits of her lover that she promises a "vingt-deux[2] under the skin" to a woman showing off.

The routine of bleeding the animals, the horrible familiarity of large knives and slaughtered animals, the nights passed in abattoirs, the sight of rats coming in the shadows to pick the remaining flesh from the skeletons—this odyssey of animal murders which once drew the admiration of Balzac serves to deaden the senses of the assassin and to imbue with sangfroid the assistant of M Deiber[3]. They kill as their day's work, and when it's done all that remains is their relief at the job done.

---

1 A secret language of butchers, where components are re-arranged.
2 Dagger in the butchers' slang.
3 The Republic's official executioner.

✳

"You should write a letter," the old woman advised the butcher Doré—"and whilst Mme Dessaignes reads it you bump her off."

Then the drama plays out. Doré scribbles on an envelope by the light of a gas lamp in a deserted street. Chotin, the youngest, who is sixteen, is made the look-out. Doré hands the letter to Mme Dessaignes: Eugène Berlant rushes at her, knocks her over, whilst the butcher bleeds her with a drill bit. Then they crush her head with the heels of their shoes. The first blow, the one which turned Mme Dessaignes into no more than a poor expiring creature, having been struck by the butcher, the only one used to attacking living beings, now young Berlant is learning his trade; he comes down whilst they're ransacking the place and stamps on Mme Dessaignes to finish her off.

It's scarcely half past eight in the evening. Their appetite for dinner had been dulled by their uncertainty about locating their victim, by the hope of loot. Now "work has given them empty stomachs". They go into the kitchen and calmly set about a supper of eggs, sardines and dried fruit, washed down with wine and rum. They give the look-out enough for his own feast and his share of thirteen sous out of twenty-three francs. Chotin doesn't complain: he's so young, and besides, he's richer than the others—since he has a "wife", Juliette Clément. (He's sixteen, she's eighteen.)

At nine o'clock they meet up with widow Berlant and Juliette, outside the Asnières theatre. "Ah! My

63

dears!" she cries, "You did a good job!" She has brought them cloth caps, a well-meaning precaution: they take off their bowler hats, and they all go to have a weep at the play, *Le Naufrage de la Méduse*[1].

Their well-deserved rest is recorded thus:

> *On Sundays I don't work*
> *I go with the kids up in the gods*
> *To watch the play or vaudeville*
> *At Belleville*

Nothing is clearer for anyone who knows assassins. These visits are typical. Supper in the kitchen is a widespread habit. Avé-Lallemant[2] presents it as characteristic. In the Auteuil affair, which featured the dreadful figure of the one-armed Sellier with his iron claw, the assassins also dined on the spot. Rarely does a theft take place, or a murder followed by theft, without the perpetrators lighting the candles, ransacking the cupboards and having a feast in the house, at the risk of getting caught. Candle ends and bits of sausage skin litter all the carpets.

But going to the theatre after committing a crime strikes a curious note in the Courbevoie affair. Doré, Berlant, Deville and Chotin, who have just kicked a poor woman to death, rush to the Asnières theatre. They

---

1 *The Shipwreck of the Medusa.*
2 Friedrich Christian Benedikt Avé-Lallemant (1809-1892), a German criminologist and author.

go to snivel over the fate of the persecuted and innocent young girl in *Le Naufrage de la Méduse*—perhaps snivelling into their checked handkerchiefs (Poe observed that real criminals always have handkerchiefs), whilst expressing their noisy disapproval of the melodrama's villain. And in a bizarre echo of that plot, when they later appear before the judge in the court of assizes, they will be convinced that they're being persecuted too, and the public-spirited words that spring to their lips will echo the literary speeches heard in their local theatres.

They are not irresponsible. They belong to a race of criminals who have their own special habits and particular instincts, so that wrongdoers across the ages all look the same, except for any differences created by historical events. The only distinctive thing about our own era is the youth of offenders. Lack of awareness, resulting from lifestyle and the corrupting lessons of their comrades, develops from a very young age. There is also a boastfulness pushing these fifteen-year-old boys to imitate their elders who have suffered and died bravely. A sort of faith, if you like, or literary admiration. Gilles and Abadie used to read the stories of Cartouche and Lacenaire in peddled editions: they will be found under their mattresses. Pranzini, Prado, Cami, Kaps, Lebiez[1] were heroes for them. "Bravo, Lebiez" cried a voice as the blade fell.

And, if the guillotine doesn't await them, they have the hope of a life far away in La Nouvelle[2], in

1 Murderers who were executed.
2 The penal colony of New Caledonia.

the Bourail colony from where occasional stories bring tales of nocturnal orgies. I have before me a letter from someone condemned to penal servitude: you could imagine it was written by Berlant, after he had appeared before the court of assizes.

> I've been had . . . You expect to get ten years, at the most: but nothing of the sort, what a difference! For me, after eight years, I still have ten to go: that's nearly twenty years. Oh, what? You think after all that time I'd want to come back? Oh no! Not that! I shall have some land, a house, a wife, some children and a dog—not to mention my poultry. Oh well—we'll have some fun at our place. There'll be parties, we'll have a good time. So let's think about that, try to kill time. I'm like you, I'm frozen; I'm dying of hunger, rage, boredom. Luckily I've got a few sous from my poor mother, poor woman . . . This is what hurts—leaving my mother. I'll stop here, you see, because it's upsetting me . . .

Don't feel sorry for him. This letter was from Charlot de Charonne; it was written in 1889 and as a signature it shows a head with a cap, a dagger, a revolver, death threats and the slogan: *Eight years' hard labour, Ten years' detention, Long live the three-card trick, Death to the cops!*

The horrible old woman who advised the murderers of Courbevoie will not be able to help her son out, since she's in prison. Berlant will not have the sadness of leaving her. And if they're not entrusted to the care of M Deibler they'll all be going to live in a prison in La Nouvelle where they'll remember their gang's exploits with the regrets demonstrated in a recent study . . .

The Execution

IN the pale darkness the gas lamps pierce the mist like stars in the night sky, a red glow from windows surrounding the Place de la Roquette—this is the setting for the death of Eyraud[1]. A restless crowd throngs the pavements of the sloping street; in the distance are muffled sounds, with the whinnying of horses. Then the silhouettes of the gendarmes appear, their boots in the stirrups as they line their horses up.

Amongst the faces in the crowd are those of the poet Rodolphe Darzens[2], gazing eagerly; and M de Winter, in the front row, his grey coat buttoned up, felt hat tilted to one side, thin moustache curling up, observing the scene with his pale eyes. Has he brought with him the generous and compassionate Russian spirit, the spirit of Turgenev who wanted to describe the execution of Troppmann[3], the spirit of Dostoyevsky with his

1 Michel Eyraud was executed on 3 February 1891 for the murder in 1889 of the court bailiff Toussaint-Augustin Gouffé; his accomplice in the crime, his mistress Gabrielle Bompard, was sentenced to twenty years' hard labour.
2 Darzens: 1865-1938, novelist and poet.
3 Jean-Baptiste Troppmann, a French mass murderer executed in

pity for the student Rodion[1]? It's hard to say.

He was present at the ablutions[2] with the imperturbability of a long-distance walker with his following of reporters like those who pursued the Wandering Jew through the driving snow. He is a gambler who has come to learn about a new way of death. In Russia they use the rope and the knout[3]; he is curious to see this method of capital punishment which is peculiar to the French, who are perhaps for him strange Occidental beings, and he will take back a clear image of a machine which, originating in the distant west, has in the past made the whole of Europe tremble.

Now the local officers are pushing back the spectators; the sky has lightened; the gas lamps are extinguished; hands are feverishly gripping the wooden barriers. There it is, the terrible machine, towering before them, narrow, its sides painted blood-red, its cap of sharp steel. The double door turns on its hinges, and there is Eyraud, a white figure in the dim light.

The yellow grease which prison spreads on the skin of convicts has run down his cheeks; his skull and high forehead shine like eggshells, with a strip of grey hair lightening towards his temples. This mysterious figure, moving rapidly forwards, strong, energetic, is reflected strangely in the gaze of those all around him; Eyraud wants to see the crowd; he has pushed the Abbé Faure away, but perhaps he is eager for the protection of men.

January 1870.
1 Raskolnikov, the hero of *Crime and Punishment*.
2 The prisoner's morning "toilette" on the day of execution, which included shaving the head and removing the shirt collar.
3 Russian scourge.

But there is the guillotine, and he is stunned and fascinated by it; he feels drawn towards it; he rushes up to it, insofar as he can, for he is tightly bound; again he pushes away the chaplain with a rough gesture, arrives at the platform and stops. Then the thoughts which have been churning inside him erupt. He was perhaps thinking about M Constans[1] when they woke him; that was the first thing he said, and he saw him, during the pitiful agony of the ablutions "decorating Gabrielle Bompard". The Minister's name comes again to his lips, in a piercing cry as he shouts: "Constans is a murderer! I'm a murderer, but Constans is a worse one!" This high-pitched sound is still floating in the air when the blade bites into flesh with a dull thud. The crowd is silent.

What a strange thought for a man staring death in the face! How easy it is to detect in the head of the former baker the jumble of incoherent ideas of a political lost sheep, the unhealthy fizzing of the gossip mongers' stories! In this cry is a mix of the rebel's hatred of society as represented by a strict minister and the defamatory attacks, the political ranting, which for him have become absolute truths; at the last moment, jealousy of Gabrielle Bompard gives way to jealousy of the guillotine.

The carriage, escorted by gendarmes, rolls rapidly in the direction of the Ivry cemetery. There, in the Turnip Field[2], the basket is emptied and the decapitated body,

1 Jean Constans (1833-1913), a politician who was French Minister of the Interior at the time.
2 Le Champ de Navets—the part of the Ivry cemetery reserved for

spattered with sawdust, is exposed to view in the pinewood coffin. By a strange chance it is face down, with the pale open hands tied behind its back; and they wedge in the head, ashen face up with its pinched and bloody nose, and closed eyelids; as if this white waxen mask is destined to spend eternity gazing backwards at the past on which Eyraud turned his back at the scaffold, thrust towards a future which this man had refused to hope for with the priest.

For he has shown himself up in all his unthinking scepticism since he failed to have Gabrielle's head roll into the basket along with his own. He no longer has any interest in his wife, or his daughter. "Be happy" is the message he sent to them. As if the weight of this cheap coffin would not crush the two poor creatures for all time.

He did not pity them; no one has pitied them. The jury's pity did not reach any further. They made a choice between the verdict and a reprieve. They opted for a definite distinction between Gabrielle and Eyraud. The flagrant discrimination in the way they were treated makes one wonder if the death penalty really was appropriate.

I have spoken here about what I find difficult to understand with this crime, the dark veil obscuring part of it, the strange reticence of certain people involved, the change of direction of the police sleuths who originally followed a different trail. This morning the police chief Goron, his nervous smile twisting his red moustache,

---

executed criminals; so called because it had previously been used for growing turnips.

seemed no longer concerned with an idea which had perhaps preoccupied him for a long time.

The man was not very interesting, agreed; he confessed, again agreed; he was condemned—yes, we can even agree on that, for you can always look at it again as long as the blade has not yet fallen. But it is a serious responsibility to pronounce the supreme sentence in the face of so many mysteries.

Eyraud killed a bailiff; we don't really know why. The bailiff Bousquet killed two people, one as vengeance, the other out of bloodthirsty cruelty. He was pardoned: and the journalist Edmond Magnier, in an impassioned article, asked why. It was a fair exchange. Bailiff for bailiff. The bailiffs' syndicate has gained one, and lost one. It won't be decorating its meeting room with a severed head. Bailiffs are hard, but so far not vengeful. If there was an appeal for clemency, I don't believe there was one for the guillotine.

So why? Was it out of love for the death penalty, which this morning the Abbé Crozes defends as "the state of grace"? That doesn't serve as a useful example for frightening ordinary wrongdoers. The Gouffé was no ordinary crime. The pendulum which started everything off and which stopped with the rope which killed Gouffé has not disappeared. This is a case, if there ever was one, for clemency, even though the two poor women in black[1] dragging themselves around at Levallois-Perret have been deliberately forgotten.

Perhaps the coming centuries, in a future we can now glimpse, will reproach us for interpreting the law's

---

1 The wife and daughter of Eyraud.

"suppression of the individual" in such a bloodthirsty way; perhaps the two red arms of the guillotine will no longer loom against a sky filled with a new light; perhaps the steel triangle, the metal garrotte and the electric chair will seem as barbarous as the copper cauldrons, the nail pincers, the boot torture, the "pears of anguish"[1], the curved iron bars and the red-hot branding irons for which our modern times unanimously stigmatise the Ancien Régime.

---

1 A medieval torture instrument.

Articles for Export

JUST as I was finishing work on *Batignolles Fashion* I saw a tall, pale, emaciated creature come in, put his hat down on the floor with a bundle of manuscripts. He murmured: "I believe you edit a fashion journal?" I replied that the issue was already finished.

Then, looking crestfallen, he picked up his hat and his papers and went to the door, putting his hand on the doorknob—as if about to leave—but then came back towards me and mumbled in a pleading tone: "Tell me, please, if you have any subscribers in the Pomotou archipelago?"

I looked at my register and read out: "Ten half-subscriptions, eighteen one-third, thirty-two quarters, seventy-two at one-eighth."

Anxiously he asked me: "Are the inhabitants not whole people?"

"Oh yes," I told him, "but they subscribe in groups."

He breathed a sigh of relief then continued quietly:

"I work in export. I have here descriptions of a fancy hat with a double veil, one part for the face, the other for the fake chignon; an advertisement for new demountable whalebone stays, and a corset with a double lower part so it can serve as a wallet, a card holder and letter carrier; an extensive article on a hinged bustle with a coil spring to make seated ladies look taller; a study promoting an excellent invention: rubber falsies in the form of a baby's bottle in which you can put all the beneficial ingredients to replace milk for young babies . . . Do you think this kind of thing would be of interest in Pomotou?"

I started to speak—he stopped me:

"You are doubtful, monsieur," he said. "Let me put you right. I spent the best years of my life in Honolulu. In Polynesia they lap up your magazines eagerly. I lost a wonderful situation through bad luck worthy of your sympathy.

"I left the provinces, monsieur, to become a writer in Paris. You must have some of my manuscripts in your basket. I have written a large amount of poetry. My poetic works cost me a great deal of effort. But the editors were not helpful. Then I published—on the off chance I must admit—a series on perfumery, tailoring and fashion. In all conscience I must accept that I never recommended a product without having tried it. My present sad situation arose from an infraction of that rule. The white stripe across my scalp is the result of trying a depilatory cream. My forehead is pitted with small holes—perhaps you can tell?—the effect of Antibolbos. Using Mammifera made me an almost supernatural being. I've worn corsets of all strengths, which destroyed my elegant figure and constricted my intestines. Almond cream reduced my hands to a formless, gelatinous state. Thanks to daily use of various rice powders I look as if I'm wearing my gloves on my face. But none of that matters, monsieur: if I had tried out the bustles[1] which caused my disaster in the Sandwich Islands[2] I would not be here.

"After putting in an enormous effort for many years I sadly had to admit that I had made no progress towards fame and fortune. My lodgings were in a miserable state. Spiders lived amongst my plates. Woodlice came out of the woodwork to marvel at my distress. Cockroaches came to make a funeral procession out of the leaves of my books. Life in Europe had become hateful to me; I decided to emigrate.

"Miserable and abandoned, I arrived at Le Havre in the rain, and embarked for Polynesia. My hatred for others led me towards cannibals. To see human flesh devoured, to hear the teeth of ferocious savages cracking the bones of the stupid readers who were leaving me to die of starvation, would be ghastly bliss.

"When I arrived at Oahu Island, entering the Honolulu roads, I felt the breeze of salvation blowing through my spirit. And when I stepped onto the soil of the Sandwich Islands I was overjoyed to think that I would be taking part in cannibalistic feasts.

"As I approached I noticed that the coconut palms carried huge gently stirring bunches of fruit. I was astonished by this extraordinary fruit. But when I came close I saw that these were human beings clinging there. Their cries filled the air. I was surrounded by these en-

---

1 Bustle: a pad or frame worn under a skirt to puff it out behind.
2 Now also known as the Hawaiian Islands.

thusiastic beings. They all had something not unknown to me. A young lady who from behind had the look of a camel because she was wearing a bustle between her shoulders and another in the small of her back rushed up to me and threw her arms round me: 'Let me, please let me, look at you,' she cried. 'How your forehead is pitted by your worries!'

"An old woman pushed her aside; she was wearing a Directoire-fashion dress split over her thighs; she covered my hands with kisses. Suddenly the truth popped into my head like a flash of lightning: it was I who had recommended this dress. The article had appeared in *Bretelle à ressorts familiale*[1]. What a low trick I had committed! Now I would always have the sight of that mottled thigh in my head.

"Then at my feet was an ocean of outdated fashions; tall hinged hats, mechanical birds on top of hats, automatic cravats, unbreakable detachable collars; a sea of paper clothing stretched before my eyes; all the men smelt of beef marrow; all the women exuded a strong perfume of mingled opopanax[2], patchouli, ylang-ylang and new-mown hay. And from the surging swells of heads, raising and lowering in turns, and carrying in their wake fancy hats, pink caps, cowboy hats, Amazonian headdresses, top hats, panama hats and bowler hats, rose hymns of thanksgiving and odes of gratitude; songs of gladness hovered in the perfumed air of the Sandwich Islands; the young girls, bulbous

---

1 "Shoulder straps with springs for all the family."
2 A fragrant gum resin used in perfumery.

in their crinolines and stiff in their mechanical corsets, burned incense as I passed. It was as if my head was touching the heavens as I entered like a monarch into Honolulu.

"I had fled from misery in Europe; I found glory in the Sandwich Islands. Yes, monsieur, at least the inhabitants of Oahu had appreciated my powerful style. In my honour they were wearing the objects I had written about. The people of the Sandwich Islands love fashion magazines. They're happy to try everything, undaunted by outlandish finery. They were seduced by my fertile imagination.

"Honolulu was for me paradise on earth. I made a mistake: I wanted to strengthen my reputation. I was keen to show these islanders how little effort it took me to produce my masterpieces. So I sent a letter to the Editor of the *Daily Shampoo* with a charming description of the new hinged bustle. But I could not try out the actual article; it was the only time I simply reported on something.

"Monsieur, the Oahu people were so enthusiastic that they ordered a whole consignment of these bustles. And as a Russian corvette had anchored off Honolulu the Russian consul gave a soirée where the ladies could show off their new bustles for the first time.

"When they got up to start dancing a dreadful detonation was heard—like the sound of fireworks—like gunfire—running fire. The Russian captain and his deputy dropped to the floor, thinking they were being blown up. In less than a moment I was surrounded, booed, threatened, vilified; two Russian sailors put me in irons. And why? Why? *Because my bustles were fraudulent. Because inside them were old hat springs.*[1]

"Monsieur, I left the Sandwich archipelago. I could not stay there. I came back to France dragging my miserable chains. But for the love of God, let me try with the people of Pomotou! Five or six articles will be enough. I would like to end my days there in peace."

Then this pale creature wiped his forehead where drops of anguished sweat had gathered. I told him that the *Batignolles Fashion* magazine did not cover Polynesian styles and gave him a letter of introduction to the *Weekly Vapouriser,* with my sincere wishes for success.

---

1 The springs used for collapsible top hats.

On Umbrellas

These few lines are taken from the intimate journal of my friend C.L.

I had an umbrella. Death took it away from me. Death carried it off at the start of its career; it was still young and no doubt one day it must have spread its wings to fly away over the high peaks; a gust of wind broke it; it is no more. I feel myself drawn towards a certain sympathy for umbrellas; I have always loved them and I'm afraid I still have something of a yen for them. That one had seduced me with its elegance, its graceful shape, its dear little ivory finial; its bones were long and narrow, its corded silk flesh shone with boundless allure and, when it opened out it floated like a real little bluestocking at the height of the ground floor windows. It didn't go up to the clouds; it avoided streams of water; it had a strange liking for dampness, it allowed you to do whatever you wished with a push of your thumb; its eight ribs gave it an acceptable expansion.

I mourn for it, for I felt it had the real spirit of an umbrella. Now with its covering hanging like a broken wing I can only think of using it for distant travels. I would have taken pleasure nevertheless in showing Italy to it, showing how a blue sky can have something sullen for those not used to it, to give it new sensations to experience. It was given to me by a "grande dame" who is often kind enough to give me dinner; and I shall try to describe for her the "snobbish" appeal of that little umbrella.

Meditation No 1.

Here is an unusual moral dilemma. I don't know whether this umbrella really belonged to the lady who gave it to me. Some people take umbrellas without really thinking. What would be the state of mind of the poor soul thus deprived of its owner?—Don't laugh: why would objects not have such upset feelings? The umbrella, historic companion of both men and women; like the lovely little terracotta bowls, positioned above Tanagra figurines or Cypriot statuettes; like big straw hats, perched on the top of heads, sunshades with living handles, and later their purple and violet canopies with their stars and gold and silver flowers; and far away, over in China and India, the canopies with their delicate green and tightly rolled ribs, which open in the sun like strolling multi-coloured cupolas—as many ancestors, as many traditions, customs, sentiments as the dim flow of heredity has brought to this umbrella.

And the setting for this? Perhaps England, first, at the end of the last century, with its deliciously *homely* feelings, the faint smell of creosote emanating exquisitely from pre-Raphaelite books, the scent of tea, the vision of small houses with small bricks, small tables, small towels, small cups, small spoons and the big *roast beefs*[1] smelling of smoke, the Oxford *fellows*, especially those of the lovely Balliol College; perhaps all that is inherent in the umbrella. Indeed, I do believe it came from England, and from a good family. (I was the one who introduced to the "grande dame"—thus earning the gratitude of her guests—dyed shirts with perfectly white cuffs, collar and shirt front; that's the English style, and the shirts arrived ready-made for me by *steamboat.*)

Meditation No 2.

Some umbrellas are big bumpkins, with copper feet, leather tassels, and made of green, red or blue cotton; there are poor umbrellas with holes where their whale-bone elbows bend, torn, with worn collars and bits of their black stalks sticking out; there are excellent umbrellas dressed in alpaca from the Magasin du Louvre or from Bon Marché, a large and decent population. Mine was not one of those; and I ascribe its "snobbery" to the awareness it had of this difference, which allows me to put forward a proposition:

Proposition No . . . *Snobbery develops in those who thanks to heredity have been endowed with refined feelings*

---

1 I.e. Englishmen.

whose setting is English, who have an interesting spirit
and who have a characteristic scorn for all that is low,
uncouth or drab.

Meditation No 3.

Umbrellas are sometimes victims of strange irrational-
ity. One day in my presence my friend C. d'O. was
telling Dr M. that he was possessed of a mania for taking the umbrellas of his best friends. Then—and this is
what is interesting about this particular psychological
quirk—he would go to a shop and have the finial of
the umbrella unscrewed and replaced. A few days later,
meeting the friend from whom he had stolen the umbrella, he would get him to admire his new acquisition,
explaining its qualities, describing its charm, getting
him to feel, caress and stroke it with his hand, tapping
his leg with its point saying, "Isn't this umbrella lovely!
I've just bought it. You wouldn't have the taste to get
one like it. Humph, yours is so coarse! Look at mine:
isn't it elegant? And soft to the touch, and light, and
well made."

Meanwhile the friend, worried, perhaps recognis-
ing his own property, was bent over C. d'O.'s umbrella
examining all its seams, but did not dare to make any
allegation because the finial was different.

This shows perversity in a very refined form. Note
that its object is not its central target but that the
object suffers nevertheless. Perhaps, thanks to us, this
mysterious depravity affects these poor souls with their

whalebone ribs. Umbrellas cannot change their own finials whenever they wish; but they can turn themselves inside out. When an umbrella is inside out it is abandoned; maybe all it wanted was to leave you. The boulevards are full of old inside-out umbrellas, with weak whalebone.

My poor little snob of an umbrella quivered in the wind like a tulip; but it didn't turn itself inside out, it got broken . . .

Meditation No 4 and final.

Reflect on the complexity of this fabric heart, made of highly esteemed metal struts and delicate silks, on its feelings which gave it vibrancy, on its aspirations towards a distant goal; imagine if it had the passion for self-analysis, for searching out its holes, for examining its whalebone ribs, for reflecting on the effects of sun and rain. Now imagine it no longer one of society's lower classes but belonging to your own, amongst the procession of elegant umbrellas resembling a vibrant avenue of multicoloured mushrooms rather than a crowd of humble melon cloches: imagine how its soul distinguishes itself from the others by the tiniest shade of difference.

But, once it is aware of itself, as one truly alone amongst umbrellas, imagine that it turns more completely in on itself; that it sees it is an umbrella, like the others, that it blushes at its shape and its being; that it wonders whether being an umbrella is truly something special when there are parasols; that it does not accept the responses of its own self-respect; that it thinks about the palaces of Florence, about the gondolas of Venice, about the well-sprung horse-drawn carriages, about everything which by its internal or external luxuriousness excludes the use of such a miserable device; then it will feel all its ribs; then it will see that its poor soul has lost all its silk canopy; then this poor soul of an umbrella will wish to leave its bodily umbrella behind, whilst rain itself will not have enough tears for its despair.

Thus, over these four meditations, I have analysed the state of mind and the "snobbery" of the poor little umbrella given to me by a very "grande dame", at whose house I dine, and I have brought it to its fatal end with its broken whalebone ribs.

Pale-Hands[1]

THE ferryman looked curiously at the two men walking down the steep path carved into the clay. The earth all around looked blood-tinged, moulded from red ochre and iron. In the distance the waves had torn into the cliffs and the sides of the bays sloped up towards the fields. The red arc of the setting sun could be seen over the sea. One of the men looked like an old tramp, and was swinging a cudgel. The other, moving with a young man's step, was whistling. They came down to the river's edge, where yellow reflections lapped at the clear green line of its bar.

Then without a word they climbed into the flat-bottomed boat and the old man stretched out his legs. The ferryman took them at an angle towards the middle of the river. The ripples shone like red and black fish scales, and the river wrapped itself like a snake around its banks. Turning to look at the other side they saw amongst the dark smudges of the waterside forests and

---

1 Translator's note: with thanks to Dr. Ken George for his help with the slang expressions in this story.

the colours of the cultivated fields a pointed wooden bridge linking the two banks amongst the fields in the far distance.

As the ferryman's boathook brought the boat up to the far bank the two men stood and proffered their cash. The bank was dark and carpeted in heather. They slowly climbed up it and disappeared over the crest. The ferryman put his oars together, pushed a stone onto the mooring chain, lit his pipe and sat down on the floor of his boat, shaking his head.

"Are you going to stop that whistling soon?" said Plague-Face.

"I'll ask your permission," replied Pale-Hands.

"You whistle and whistle; anyone would think you like being on the road."

"Maybe I do."

Plague-Face sat down on a mound.

"That's enough," he said, "I'm not walking any further. Not here, not there. My dogs are barking and my head's splitting. That's it, no more walking, do you hear?"

"I'm still standing," said Pale-Hands.

He leaned back against a low earth wall, pulled a piece of sausage out of his pocket and started calmly nibbling it, carefully peeling off the skin.

Plague-Face watched him for a few minutes

"Anyway, where did you get that bit of old leather?"

"That, old man," said Pale-Hands, "is my business. It's got nothing to do with you."

"Where did you pinch it?"

"Pinch?" said Pale-Hands. "As if you're not the one to go nicking things? I don't go stealing."

"No, but you're happy to scoff what I get for you."

"Something wrong with that?" said Pale-Hands.

There was a silence. Then Plague-Face started up again.

"Don't think you can take me in, Pale-Hands. I've still got all my marbles. You got that bit of old leather from that dead loss of a boy you've been shagging in town."

"So?" said Pale-Hands. "It's none of your business."

"No, but just see if I don't slip him a length myself one day."

"Huh! He'll rip your guts out, more like, old man. Have you looked at yourself in the mirror? You're over a hundred years old. You're bald as an egg. Nobody would have you for the fun of it."

"Okay, you could find better," said Plague-Face.

"Anyway," continued Pale-Hands, "you know, if you don't like it . . . We're not married. So go your own way, I'll go mine. I don't want to get nicked because of you. If the cops nab you, I'll send you something in the nick."

"Oh yes?" said Plague-Face. "So was it me that passed on those dud coins at the baker's and the butcher's? Was it me who took those lead five-franc pieces to the bistro to pay for drinks for all the mates? Was it me who bought plaster, fancy footwarmers, charcoal, wax, iron scoops?"

"Oh yes?" said Pale-Hands. "So was it me who learnt from an old geezer like you? Was it me who asked you to fake the phoney dough? Was it me who pinched a hundred sous to pay for stuff? Wasn't it Plague-Face— oh! no—who tempered the mixture, beating it and heating the tin, and the copper, and the silver paper, so the window of my digs glowed red at night and the landlord wanted to throw us out?"

"Shut up," cried Plague-Face, "I remember the house in the rue St Denis where everything was going so well your knife stayed the whole evening on the table."

"And you, you old crook," cried Pale-Hands, "how many murders have you got on your conscience?"

Plague-Face went towards his companion, hands raised, then stopped and said:

"You're not worth it. You go your way, I'll go mine."

Pale-Hands shrugged, started whistling again, and set off along a path which crossed the road.

Plague-Face picked up his truncheon and continued on the main road, prodding the heaps of stones with his stick in the darkness.

And suddenly he felt very old and alone, that he hadn't eaten, that he would never again hear Pale-Hands' voice nor see his face. With his comrade he'd had fun leading the police a merry dance. Alone on this unknown road he almost wished he was back in his cell. There was no moon that night. Winter was coming on. His steps echoed on the hard ground. From the distant sea came the murmur of the surf. Plague-Face had thought that he and his companion would play the three-card trick in the villages and that they would sleep by the fire when it rained, having played with the wagon drivers and bought drinks for the pub landlords. Being old, alone, looking dreadful, feelings of deep distress came over him.

The road wound round a dark hill. Plague-Face fell to the ground, muttered into his beard and fell asleep.

The sky's small cold clouds turned pink in the rising sun and the old fugitive shivered in the five o'clock wind. He was lying close to an old ruined wayside cross; and when he stood up he saw someone sleeping on the other side of it. Plague-Face recognised Pale-Hands who had been led to this same crossroads by a side path. The light of dawn made his skin look even paler and his half-open young lips were as if milk-softened. Sleep had taken away Plague-Face's irritation but left him the sadness of the previous evening. For a moment he wanted to shake Pale-Hands and resume his wicked way of life with him. But he passed his hand over his bald head; Pale-Hands dozed on, as if innocently. He remembered the sermons preached to prisoners, stating that the young could be cured of criminality, believed that this village's wayside cross was there for a reason, imagined that he knew on which side of it the wicked criminal had slept, shook off his fatigue and continued on his way along the murky road.

Possessed by the Devil

THE table had been set up under the trees and the embroidered cloth was strewn with dead leaves. A few of them floated on the champagne in its narrow glasses. Only one candle was left, and around it you could hear the buzzing of insects. The guests had moved away. The sound of voices occasionally reached this thicket. Anxiously I wandered around, dreaming of that mysterious person, then suddenly I started back for there she was, sitting amongst the ice buckets and the silver bowls. She was shaking with inner laughter. Her face was lit by a tall orange-coloured lantern hanging from a branch. I saw her ankles twitching, tightly wrapped in a golden mesh. Her dress clung to her hips and rippled over her breasts like the pale milky surface of a pond, its fabric the delicate colour of a migrant mantis. Then I noticed her hands, clasped together. Suddenly the muscles of her neck quivered. Her mass of hair twisted; her eyes widened and became fixed; her mouth opened, wide and red. This trembling happened three times, and she seemed to want to speak. But she could not, for her pulsating lips would not close and her throat seemed constricted. The third time, shaking her head, she let out a hoarse cry, wrung her hands, played knucklebones with some pieces of ice and broke a champagne flute with her teeth. Suddenly she lifted her skirt, stretched a leg with its strange wrapping of gold filigree towards the candle and crushed it. The orangey glow vanished. Then I heard her sigh with pleasure.

I don't know this woman's name, nor where she comes from; nor even whether she is beautiful; I know she is possessed by a demon which harasses her. Daniel Defoe wrote of Moll Flanders that after spending thirty years as a prostitute on the streets of London she was without shelter and without money. As she passed an open shop where the salesgirl with her back turned to the street was looking at a display shelf by the light of a candle, Moll Flanders saw a white package on a chair. And a demon came up behind her and whispered in her ear: "Take that package: take it quickly, take it." She took it and fled. Then she wept beneath the arch of a bridge over the Thames. Now that demon is wriggling its gold-wrapped legs, breaking crystal glasses in its teeth, and spreading itself voluptuously on tables where people have dined, amongst the bowls with their sparkling chilled wine. And the woman wants to weep: but only laughter comes to her lips, and the protest sticks in her throat.

I'm sure I've seen her before. It was at a town on the coast where a long dusty, roughly paved road leads to the sea. At the end of it, at intervals through the line of slate rooftops, you can see the masts, the multicoloured pennants floating in the wind and the taut halyards. Around my mid-life I had lost all my money, having more than once enjoyed dining beneath the trees. With my grey beard, and my rucksack on my back, I was walking along the road leading to the Western Ocean, with the intention of earning my bread on a ship. Some of the houses were painted red and blue, and above the gables, where you sometimes see a holly branch waving, heads of negro women and tropical birds had been carved. The shutters were closed; from the half-open doors came the sound of rhythmical footsteps, the gasps of dancers amongst the scraping of violins and the chinking of glasses being carried in the cool darkness. In the window of a small shop there was a copper plate. I pushed the door and saw three sailors sitting near a strange-looking female barber. She was wearing a short skirt and her legs and arms were covered in black tattoos. She was silently soaping their faces and shaving them all in the same way. When she had finished, the three sailors put on their yellow oilskin capes and kissed her on the cheek, though she did not reciprocate. They left and the barber came towards me holding her razor, without a word. Then she was seized by a fit of trembling, her head jerking; her mouth opened three times like the steel drawer of a machine. And at the third time the cry which issued from her lips did not match her body at all, so I thought another person was speaking through her. With the door closed and the curtains drawn, she soaped my beard, hair and eyebrows in the darkness; I felt the cold metal sliding over my skin. And I yielded, knowing an unknown someone was in charge. And when I escaped with my shaved head, smooth like that of a foreign penitent, I could see her laughing, slashing at her arms with the edge of the razor, sniffing delightedly at her own blood.

And now I'm afraid. For I shall have to see her again. She was golden in my happy days, black in my misery—how will she look at my end? I have sought her on oriental shores, in flower-covered junks, in small sand houses, in square holes in the rock where the prostitutes live in foreign countries like flocks of evil birds. Amongst those women who eat fire and glass, and those who pierce their arms and cheeks with ivory pins, and those who drive turquoises into the wounds in their foreheads—not one of them has come to me. In which witches' sabbath shall I find her again and what will be the final punishment imposed on me by the demon which possesses her?

Blackbeard

WE had left Jamaica at the end of March 1717, with a fine cargo of quinquina[1] and rum. Our plan was as we progressed along the coast to buy various exotic fruits and to resell them on the islands where they were not grown, such as guava, papaya, yellow mombins, juniper berries, combava and cashew fruits, amongst which none is better than the naseberry which is the size of a pear with crimson flesh. The master of our sloop, the *Adventure,* was David Harriott, and on board were two good-time girls, Spaniards, whom we called Machilla and Machillon. They knew the country well, moving from one inn to another, helping the sailors to drink their rum, each of them wearing on their breast a small purse of stitched leather full of pieces of eight.

On the evening of 9 April, off Turneffe Island, ten leagues from the bay of Honduras, running before a strong breeze, we suddenly saw a sloop at anchor, close to a large ship like those which transport cheapjack

---

1 An aperitif made with quinine.

goods in Guinea. And scarcely had the *Adventure*'s master ordered the deck to be cleared and the cannon holes to be opened than the smoke of cannon fire spewed out of the large vessel to starboard; upon which the unknown sloop hoisted a black flag and sped towards us. Machilla and Machillon cried upon all the Spanish saints and berated each other for their sins; but Captain David drew his pistols and from the movement of his lips we understood that he was telling us to take up our arms against the pirates: for the sound of his voice was immediately lost amongst the dreadful racket of several horrific bottles full of gunpowder and pieces of iron exploding in the yards and the sails and against the bulwarks. Through the thick smoke, before any of us had had the chance to grab a musket or a sword, men rushed towards us like devils, swearing at the tops of their voices; and the sight of one of them, even more devilish than the others, had the two Spanish girls swooning. His black beard reached down to the middle of his chest and up towards his eyes, its tresses braided into pigtails tied with ribbons hooked over his ears; his face was completely smeared with soot; he held a cutlass in his teeth and a pistol in each hand and four bigger pistols clashed together in their sheaths above his gunpowder bag as they swung from a sash like a bandolier hanging from his shoulders. And from below two of the points of his cocked hat hung the red glow of lighted harquebus fuses. This was how, through the fog from his diabolical exploding bottles, we saw for the first time Blackbeard the Pirate[1].

---

1 A historical character, Edward Teach or Edward Thatch (c. 1680-

We were tied up and thrown into the sloop, and kicked along the side of the large warship with its forty cannons, the *Revenge*[1], above which floated the black flag with its death's head wearing a three-cornered hat. On the deck stood Captain Blackbeard, the two fuses still smoking with a dreadful smell of scorching hat. In a voice hoarse from drinking rum, he ordered us in his English jargon to tell him where our money was. Machilla and Machillon crossed themselves: so that the men saw their little leather bags and snatched them away mercilessly. Master David had his thumbs tied with a fuse which they set fire to; but he wasn't able to give away any hiding place. When his howls became too loud Blackbeard slashed his neck with his cutlass, impatiently pulling at his hair. Then he turned to the other pirates and licked the blood from his blade and its handle. My throat went dry with horror. They put a plank onto the boom and each of the sailors from our poor sloop had to run along it, prodded by sword points, until they jumped into the sea and disappeared beneath the waves.

As for me, as I was young Blackbeard kept me as his servant, and Machilla and Machillon he kept to give to his men after the rum distribution, which took place amongst great pandemonium. Then straightaway he kicked me into the opening of a hatchway, and followed me down. He made me braid his beard, which

---

1718), better known as Blackbeard, an English pirate who operated around the West Indies and the eastern coast of Britain's North American colonies.
1 Blackbeard's ship was actually called *Queen Anne's Revenge*.

he greased with coconut oil, all the time swearing non-stop. Then he took a small book with a parchment cover, in which he made a number of crosses with a quill pen, crushing its nib in his rage. I thought he was keeping his logbook and this is what he wrote:

> *Yesterday all the rum finished—ship's company going hungry—a damned brawl— the scoundrels are plotting—blathering about separation—keeping an eye out for booty—today pillaged a boat laden with rum—kept the company nice and warm, bloody warm—all going well.*

When he had finished, after about half an hour, in between the crosses, stains and dashes with which he covered the page, he began firing his pistol across the cabin, with his arm now bent, now straight, or with his eyes closed. Each time I jumped, terrified by the whistling bullets and the acrid smoke of gunpowder, thinking at any moment I would be shot dead, he opened his mouth as if to laugh.

Then he drank some rum, straight from a cask full of liquor which he kept there. And then the idea came to him for a strange invention which would be our salvation. Climbing up to the deck he shouted:

"My friends, we're all damned, and as we're all going straight to hell I want to see it, hell and damnation, before I get there. Pots of sulphur and saltpetre with fuses, down in the bilges, d'you hear? Light them, light them! I'll have my own hell!"

And shouting this he chased me with the flat of his sword, and Machilla and Machillon too, to the far end of the poop where the small boat was wobbling on its frame. And when the pirates had gone down into the hold, all the hatches were closed. Then, despite my terror, I made a sign to the two exhausted girls. I undid one of the knots holding the little boat and let the mooring rope run through my fingers. The boat fell at such a speed that the rope cut into my palm. But the boat hit the water without capsizing; and using the same rope we slid along the side of the ship. As we brushed past the keel we heard Captain Blackbeard howling:

"This is hell! Smoky, red and stinking hell! Bloody hell! Bloody hell! We'll never stand it. Damn your bloody eyes! Open the portholes!"

The portholes opened and through the illuminated slits an ominous burst of sulphur poured into the night air.

Our boat drifted away; and soon the *Revenge* was a black mass with glimmers of green and yellow. That was the last I knew of Blackbeard.

Now I travel around the inns, in the countryside, with Machilla and Machillon. It's true, they were a bit damaged by the pirates; but they still have their red lips, and I have attached to my belt two new little leather purses which they fill every day with pieces of eight.

The "Reds" in Basle (1430)

BASLE was a Republic and a free city, governed by an assembly of eminent men, a consul and a bishop; it was a discreet and courteous city, sitting on the banks of the lower Rhine, with its little conical houses roofed with fluted ribbed tiles, its multitude of small moulded barred windows, its pepper-pot turrets with their blue and yellow painted roofs, its old wooden bridge and its neat monastery like a scarlet mist where St George plunges his blood-stained spear into the jaws of the red sandstone dragon.

The city jutted like a pier into the encircling waters of the wide, green, lustrous Rhine, between the distant snow-covered mountains and tiny Basle hills, the Leonardberg, the Kohlemberg and the Munsterberg, where the steep streets climbed with their colourful shop signs—the rue de Heaume and the rue de la Couronne, the rue de Cygnes and the rue de l'Homme Sauvage, near to the fish market and the stone lion spouting its jet of pure water like a crystal arc.

There were respectable inns where girls with round cheeks poured clear wine into pewter jugs, where priests' robes and capes hung as pledges; the Town Hall where bourgeois gentlemen wearing their cloth capes, their shirts of unbleached linen, with their gold rings on their second fingers, dispensed prompt justice to wrongdoers, and around the Consuls' Building the peaceful narrow streets with their scribes' booths equipped with parchments and writing desks; calm women with moist blue eyes, their faces worn with caring, their double chins, their white linen wimples, their mouths sometimes hidden behind a strip of fine cloth; young girls in white dresses with sleeves slashed at the elbows and cherry-coloured belts, who seemed to have wrapped their long hair around spindles; red-headed children with pale lips.

In this deadly calm the master painters of Basle, having studied in Haute Alsace or in Swabia, portrayed rigid Christs, their beards sodden with the sweat of their death agony, the wounds in their sides and their hands the colour of violets, stretched out on the tomb's catafalque wrapped in their pale winding sheets; and they covered the walls of the parish churches with dreadful frescoes showing Death with his sinister hood, beating the soldier's drum, snatching up the naked child, shaking the monk's lantern, biting the lips of a fat woman, his foot on a king's orb, astride the sceptre between his thigh bones.

And the townspeople seemed to be thinking of their small cemetery, surrounded by shops, and of their charnel-house where the painters went to copy the shiny iron fittings, the greenish hands of the dead and their grinning skulls. Beneath the narrow gables of their houses the burghers had engraved:

MORITURO SAT[1]

thus testifying to the fact that they awaited with resignation and humility their transfer to the other communal residence.

Such was the liberty acquired and conserved by the inhabitants of Basle when the town was surprised by free-spirited people coming from another place.

An unknown number of them spread throughout the countryside—beggars, epileptics, crying St Anthony's Fire[2] and carrying the scallop shell of St James of Compostela. Their language was incomprehensible. They called themselves *Roten* or *Reds* and claimed that a *Red*, according to their customs, was free and emancipated in all societies.

The *granteners*[3] came to the church entrance at the end of services, falling onto the pathway, their mouths frothing with soap foam, their nostrils bleeding from being pricked with straws; or with bloody cloths fixed to their foreheads, pretending to be wounded; or with faces smeared with a product simulating burns. The *valkentreiger*[4] made circular lacerations on their arms

1 "For one about to die, it is enough."
2 A dreaded illness, common in the Middle Ages, characterised by intense inflammation of the skin.
3 Beggars pretending to be ill.
4 "Falcon carriers"—so-called because of simulated wounds to their arms.

and hands as if they had been in chains or shackles and praised St Nicholas for their deliverance. There were those whose scam was to produce fake documents as proof of being a ruined merchant, and others pretending to be priests uncovered their heads to show false tonsures. The *spanfelders*[1] left their old clothes at the hostelry and wept naked beneath the porches of churches; the blind beggars hid their round caps and begged for others until they had a wealth of dozens of hats; those pretending to be mad danced and gesticulated with crazy gestures; the grovellers said they'd been executioners and howled their contrition.

Amongst the women those pretending to be with child plumped up their waistlines with old padded jackets beneath their petticoats until they looked pregnant; and those pretending to be repentant prostitutes wandered through the villages as if freed from their own bodies, begging for alms for the love of St Mary Magdalene . . . Some of them peeled mushrooms, smeared them with blood, and placed them on their chests, then complained of having ulcerated breasts.

They played a dice game they called *riblinge*, stole *breitfuss* and *flughart*, or geese and hens, and their den was the *sonnewboss* or brothel. They demanded *liebriche*, *lem* and *johan*—women, bread and wine— and feared only being *gebricket in der gabal*, or arrested in the town; for justice condemned old robbers to be drowned (*floeessen*) and the young ones to having their ears chopped off (*das sniden der luselinge*).

---

1 People begging for clothes.

Several of these Reds, or free spirits, were taken to the Basle Consuls' House, which they greatly insulted, calling it *arseposse* and *sefelbosz*[1], which in their language indicates "rubbish dump". They laughed at the consul and the townspeople, publicly mocking the death paintings.

The free citizens were not at all pleased about the liberties taken by the free spirits. A few were captured and thrown in sacks into the green waters of the Rhine, from the height of the Old Bridge; the others fled via the St Alban and St John gates. Out on the open road they became *Reds* again. The Basle townsfolk continued with their peaceful free way of life. They made a ruling against the free spirits, a copy of which can be seen in the book of statutes in the town's archives.

---

1 Clearly very rude medieval German slang . . .

Nidau

NEAR BIEL[1], just above its lake with its dark green choppy waters and dismal rushes dipping down, I noticed a square tower with a tiled roof and a huge red coat of arms on which a furious-looking black bear[2] climbed up a yellow diagonal stripe, its jaws gaping.

The rain obscured the bushes, crackled in the furrows; a cold mist covered the mountains of the Jura, their menacing slopes bristling with black pine trees and slim red beeches, as if painted with darkness and streaked with blood. A narrow rusting train track ran up through the clay along a trench from the gorge, between the dark clumps of trees and the patches of snow. Rain dripped like tears from the corners of the heavy tarpaulins covering small abandoned wagons. Gusts of wind whistled over the greenish eddies of the lake, bending the reeds, rippling the cloudy mud pools.

There was a small old house there, huddled beneath its roof, and behind its twisted tiles, sleeping amongst

---

1 Now also known as Bienne (in the Canton of Bern, Switzerland).

2 A black bear has been shown on the Bern coat of arms since the twelfth century.

the dust, were small books printed on rough paper, decorated with ancient engravings on plain wood. This was how I re-read the stories of *Little Red Riding Hood, The Little Sister and Little Brother, Poor Henry* and the sad tale of *Snow-White*, where there is a talking looking-glass. And I also read the adventure of the three who arrived from the other side of the Rhine.

BALLAD

> *There were three who came from beyond the Rhine.—Came to stay with the hostess.— Hostess, do you have beer and wine?—Where is your little white daughter?*
>
> *My beer is cold, my wine is clear.—My daughter is lying on a stretcher.—They entered the bedchamber—saw her lying on black boards.*
>
> *The first one lifted the sheet—and looked at her sadly;—beautiful girl, if you still lived—I would love you from this day on.*
>
> *The second threw off the sheet—and turned away in tears;—alas, to see you lying there—so many years I have loved you.*
>
> *The third lifted the sheet—and kissed the pale mouth;—I have always loved you, and today I love you—and I shall love you for all eternity.*

When I had finished reading the ballad I stopped looking at the little books of rough paper with their red and green index tabs and thought about the old tower with its coat of arms and its dreadful bear.

"Ah, that's Nidau," an old peasant-woman said to me as she passed, wrapped in a cloak.

I went on along the wild yellow muddy path as far as Lake Biel. There, where the lake disappears into a lush green swamp, still frothing it empties into the Ziehl with a small current that is just enough to turn the mill wheel.

To get into Nidau I went beneath two small projecting turrets, whose windows with stone latticework seemed not to have looked on anything for many years.

And straight away I had a great surprise.

The little houses, fortified like dragons of old with scales of painted zinc, had collapsed. In the open square three fountains were enclosed in low walls of shiny stone, with smart ironwork and the jaws of beasts from which a trickle of water dripped. An ancient inscription forbade the muddying of the well waters and promised a reward of half the fine to anyone reporting a miscreant. Above the barber-surgeon's stall a jagged copper plaque banged against the green shutters with its legend, written in bloody letters, that the master barber-surgeon carries out bloodletting, drains abscesses and pulls teeth:

ADER LASSEN
GESCHWUERE HEILEN
ZAEHNE ZIEHEN

An old carriage, missing its insides, waited in the shed of a hostelry with its camp beds and pewter pots. All the tiles, embedded in lead, seemed to be looking curiously inwards, towards the past. Small children, around the wells, were playing at hopscotch. At the far end of the square, in a sort of alcove of this fifteenth-century dormitory, the church's strange red clock tower, pointed as a square dagger, leaned at an angle of eighty degrees.

I found the pastor—*Herr Pfarrer*—at the top of a house with high arches, where the staircase spiralled on and on with its massive ornate handrail. His small room was bare, grey. His books in Latin and Hebrew, poorly bound and with yellowed labels, covered one wall. He was sitting near his narrow bed of scrubbed walnut. He had gold-rimmed spectacles and a greying beard.

Handing over the three large keys to the chapel— for he had a parochial funeral service at midday—he complained mildly, with a weak smile, that Nidau and his chapel tower which leaned at a dangerous angle were built on stilts amid the green waters of Lake Biel.

Inside the little church was a brown wooden pulpit; with its stiff, rigid appearance and austere decoration, its hard pews with their unused doors hanging from their hinges, its imperial look, it served the Landvogt[1] and his family, the bailiff of the German Empire.

The Empire's coat of arms, carved into the stone of one of the portals of the bailiff's castle like the imprint of a hot iron, shows a lion carrying a globe and a cross whilst another lion cuts through the air with its sword.

---

1 Provincial governor.

On the square tower the black bear of Bern rushes towards its freedom.

This is the Nidau prison, where poor vagabonds dream about the white road on the other side of its two-feet high locks with their ornamental bolts, their huge coils, fixed to the worm-eaten wood of the pointed doorways. The gaoler was trampling the pigswill for his pigs and was not to be disturbed. I was guided beneath the vaults by a small tow-headed boy and his Spitz dog with its pointed muzzle, its ruff of black and white fur at its throat and its quivering curled tail.

The wind moaned around the pointed and round windows, around the arrow slits, along the wooden steps, and nudged the large red and black painted shutters.

The lad reached up to press down the catch on the huge lock of the last fortified chamber, releasing a torrent of cold air.

The Spitz was sitting at the corner of a step.

"Are you afraid here?"

"*Nei,*" replied the child.

"Do you come up here with your dog?"

"*Jo,*" he said.

"And what's your little friend's name?"

"*Blaess.*"

All these questions elicited just those three monosyllables.

Beneath the main beams of the mighty roof, lit by the hostile arrow slits through which could be seen the black Jura and the green Lake Biel, stretched the icy-cold long torture chamber, with the impressive breaking wheel on which the bailiff would tie his prisoners to pieces of wood with still rotting ropes.

Beyond one of the painted shutters, scarcely visible through the thick iron bars, I picked out the wretched face of a prisoner.

The Spitz trotted along the steps.

The wind howled through the arrow slits.

And then I was trampling the yellow mud outside the castle, by its sheds and outbuildings. When I turned, for a long time I could still see the narrow torrent of the Ziehl, the foaming green water of Lake Biel, and the black bear climbing the square tower of Nidau.

The Hand of Glory[1]

DEPOSITION of the maidservant:
I, Nancy, around twenty-five years of age,
kitchen hand at the hostelry of the Old Hospital in
Muir on the moors, swear by the holy book to reveal
the whole truth about the attack in December 18**,
and declare the following:

In winter we take in very few travellers, as the moorland is scattered with grey stones and heathers, and
mud-filled holes; so that the wagon drivers only rarely
come through Muir, and those who cross the moor
on foot fear the terrible winds which blow up there as
Christmas approaches. That Tuesday evening the milk
froze in the pails and after Doll and I had brought it
into the kitchen we stayed sitting by the mantelpiece
where Master Douglas—old Doug, as we called him—
was roasting potatoes in a pan before going to bed. We
were calmly spending the evening like this, with old
Doug, his wife Mistress Elisabeth, and John, the stable
lad. There were no travellers at the inn.

---

1 A Hand of Glory is the dried and pickled hand of a male person
who has been hanged, often specified as being the left hand, or, if
the man was hanged for murder, the hand that "did the deed".

About ten o'clock everyone felt tired; but I wanted to finish knitting an armband for the sick child of Mistress Dorothea, the Mistress's sister, who lives at the corner of the street. Old Doug took away the candle: for the logs in the hearth gave enough light for me to work by and I was so used to the movement of the needles that my fingers could do the knitting by themselves.

So I was dreaming, by the flickering red light of the fire, and I had promised Doll I would soon come to join her, as when it is really cold we share a bed. I could hear the crackling of the path; and the whippoorwill[1] called several times in the darkness. Suddenly I heard footsteps and a knock at the door. At first I shook with fear: it could have been midnight and they say the black King hunts at that time on the Muir moorland.

At the second knock, I summoned my courage and lifted the catch, and amid the hurricane of drizzle and fine hailstones I saw a shivering woman, her hands white with the cold.

In a serious voice she asked for shelter and a mug of beer; she offered to sleep on the floor of the hallway, promising to leave at daybreak. As soon as she was seated she put between her feet, beneath her skirt, a canvas bag full of old clothes, and gazed into the fire. I drew a mug of beer: my hands were so numb with cold that I spilled nearly half as I brought it to her.

Then I took up my knitting again and continued with my work, for the eyes of this woman frightened me a little and I dared not leave her there in the main room. But sleep overtook me, and my head jerked up

---

1 Nightjar.

now and then. Once, as my eyelids closed, I noticed the hem of this woman's skirt—and jerked awake. I had seen a man's trousers beneath it.

Shivers ran up my spine, but I kept still, pretending to be asleep. The fake woman looked around, came over to examine me carefully, then undid the bag and took out of it a dried and withered dead man's hand. She stuck a candle into it, lit it at the fire, and passed it two or three times under my nose, saying:

"Let those who sleep, sleep; let those who are awake stay awake."

Then she blew out the candle, and fixed the white hand into the copper candle holder which old Doug had left on the table; she smeared the dead fingers with oil and lit the hand at the fire. Four fingers flamed; but she could not get the thumb to burn. Then she seemed anxious, listened, without moving, and looked at me. Then the fake woman made up her mind, whistled, opening the door and called out into the night:

"Harman! Gole!"

There were two whistle blasts and voices replied:

"We're coming! We're coming!"

I rushed towards the door, pushed it with all my strength and drew the bolt; then I turned to the dreadful dead hand and tried to blow out the flames: they were coming up towards my face. I tipped the mug of beer over the hand: the flames leapt, crackling. Then I ran towards the staircase, shouting:

"Master Douglas! Mistress Elisabeth! Doll! John!" There was no movement. I leapt to Doll's bed and shook her: waste of time, for the hand still flamed.

Meanwhile they were banging violently on the door, yelling insults:

"Open up, you whore, we're going to bleed you dry. Are you going to open up? We'll break the door down and roast your head on the fire. Are you going to open up, whore? Answer! We know you're awake, since the thumb won't burn. Answer! Are you going to open up?"

Pale with fright I backed towards the kitchen and tripped against the bucket of milk. I grabbed it and poured the thawed milk onto the flaming hand. It crackled and went out.

At the same time I heard Doll shouting, and old Doug jumping out of bed on hearing the tumult. He fired his musket out of the window. There was a groan, then silence, and then a voice cried:

"The Hand! The Hand of Glory!"

But as soon as Doll was awake I ran to her bed; I hid against her and burst into tears. Old Doug threw the horrible hand into the fire, where it burned up straightaway. He and John, armed with muskets, followed the traces of blood by torchlight as far as a hole in the ground of the moor.

Rampsinit

AFTER spending one night with the master thief who in the morning had held out the dead hand of a corpse to her[1], Ahouri, the daughter of King Rampsinitos, had fallen in love. She asked her father to allow her to marry the man to whom she had voluntarily surrendered her virginity. And the old king, who admired the thief, consented; and he left to the thief his throne and his treasure in the paved chamber with the loose brick. The thief became King of Egypt and was called Rampsinit.

A short time later Queen Ahouri became ill with a painful forehead. The magicians kneaded lumps of clay with dried herbs and wrote charms in black and red

---

1 The background to this is as follows: The master thief and his brother had robbed the King's treasury together, by removing a brick which had deliberately been left loose by their father, the keeper of the treasure, but the brother had become trapped and begged his own brother to decapitate him, which he did. Later he took away one of the corpse's arms. The King's daughter had been set to discover the culprit by sleeping with clients of the royal brothel, but when she tried to grab the arm of the master thief, having inveigled the truth out of him, he had thrust the dead arm at her and fled.

ink, and stroked Ahouri's nostrils with plants gathered under the full moon, in accordance with the recommendations in the book of Imhotpou. But the Queen's body became covered in pink blotches and she had fits of shivering. And the doctors consulted the book of Thot, then shook their heads.

During the following night a great cry went up in the middle of the palace. The embalmers arrived with the sunrise, carrying three golden coffins; and the women washed Ahouri and turned the back of her head towards the south. Then a prayer was said and the first operative broke into her skull[1] using a sharp hook inserted through her left nostril. Then a prayer was said and the scribe used his reed pen to draw a black line along the left part of the abdomen. Then a prayer was said and the opener used his Ethiopian obsidian knife to cut along the line. Then the slaves rushed on him, hitting him with sticks; for his function is an unclean one. And the inside of the corpse was washed with palm wine and the innards plunged into a barrel of natron[2].

Straightaway the soul of Queen Ahouri left through her lips and fled towards the Opening of the Mouth[3] through which one descends to the goddess Hathor. And all the members of the household cried: "To the West! To the West!"[4]

---

1 I.e. to remove the brain.
2 An embalming solution.
3 The ancient Egyptians believed that in order for a person's soul to survive in the afterlife it would need to have food and water. The opening of the mouth ritual was thus performed so that the person who died could eat and drink again in the afterlife.
4 I.e. the Kingdom of the Dead, over which the goddess Hathor, one of the principal Egyptian deities, ruled.

After the necropolis workers had draped the embalmed queen in garlands to lay her to rest in the chamber of plain stone, and the last trowel of the masons had tapped against the brick wall, King Rampsinit was filled with grief. And knowing that the soul of his dear Ahouri now lived freely in the Isle of Souls, amid the unknown Ocean, he said to himself:

"I stole from King Rampsinitos the treasure of the paved chamber, I shaved the right cheeks of the palace guards and I stole from them the headless body of my brother; I left Princess Ahouri with a corpse's hand and arm; why should I not now steal from the goddess Hathor what belongs to me?"

And he set off towards the West, leaving the royal sailboat and its oarsmen by the bank of the Nile. And a long time later he arrived in a silted land, strewn with mud huts. It was the edge of the great desert. A dishonest innkeeper saw him passing and cried:

"Wouldn't you like a beer?"

And King Rampsinit entered the hut. The innkeeper, with a sideways look, put a jug of beer in front of him and said,

"Are you not the famous Rampsinit?"

But the King did not wish to answer. Then the innkeeper eyed the royal *uraeus*[1] (which Rampsinit had hidden inside his clothes so that he could be protected without being recognised) and went on:

"You are yourself the famous thief Rampsinit, and I will help you; for I am a thief myself and I admire you greatly."

---

1 The cobra at the front of a pharaoh's crown, symbolising royal power and protecting the wearer.

Then he drank beer with the King.

And the King slept that night on a bed of dried earth. When the line of sand in the distance came into view, the innkeeper said to him:

"Listen, your journey is a dangerous one. You will be crossing a shifting gorge and beyond it is a sycamore, growing in the sand. You must wait at the foot of the sycamore; and a goddess will raise towards you through the foliage half her naked body, and will offer you a dish of bread and a bowl of water. If you accept you will become her guest in the eternal abode, and you will not be able to return; if you refuse you will not be able to descend into the valley of death: for there you must pass through torrents of boiling water where monstrous monkeys fish for the souls of the dead in their nets."

"I accept," said the King, "and I shall not be her guest."

"Then she will lead you through the Opening of the Mouth into the soul of the necropolis; and she will invite you to play *Fifty-two*[1] on the sarcophagus of the Queen. If you lose you will stay buried inside the necropolis; if you win all you will get is a golden towel."

"I shall play," said the King, "and I shall win."

The innkeeper smiled and said,

"You are the famous thief Rampsinit. You are the stronger. Hathor's towel is a magic one. If you wipe your face in front of Ahouri without feeling desire you will be all-powerful, and you will be able to take away

---

1 Game of draughts in which the pieces sometimes were in the shape of dogs' heads.

those you choose from the underworld; but if you do not experience renunciation disaster will befall you."

"Holding the golden towel," said the King, "I shall feel no desire."

So Rampsinit set off, and he found the sycamore on the sand. And a goddess with painted breasts appeared through the foliage, with a twig of myrtle between her teeth, to offer him the dish of bread and the bowl of water. And Rampsinit, crouching, poured the water over his shoulder and threw the bread with his clever fingers into a fold of his robe.

Straight away the goddess led him into a bare chamber. The King saw Ahouri's sarcophagus; and he recognised her heavy golden mask and her blue-painted hair. Hathor was crouching in front of him, and they moved the pieces around on the red and green draughtboard.

Rampsinit lost the first game—and Hathor put the board on his head and he sank into the paving stones of the necropolis up to his thighs.

"Dare you go on playing?" she said.

"Yes," replied the King.

And he lost the second game, and Hathor put the board on his head, and he sank into the paving stones of the necropolis up to his waist.

"Dare you go on playing?" she said.

"Yes," replied the King.

And whilst Hathor glanced sideways preparing for the next throw of the dice, Rampsinit stole twelve pieces from the goddess. Thus he won the third game, and Hathor released him from the paving stones using her magic words.

They embarked on a boat which moved of its own accord, and arrived at the Field of Beans.

And there the precious towel hung from a sycamore branch. The goddess took it, and Rampsinit covered his face with it.

Suddenly he saw his dear Ahouri amongst the ears of wheat seven cubits high, saw her clearly through the golden veil. And, looking through its lower part, he could see one of her white feet and her ankle encircled with turquoises. And, forgetting everything, he desired to grasp this foot, as Ahouri had grasped the hand of the dead man on the night he had first taken her, so that he could steal her once again.

Straightaway blackness entered his eyes and disaster was upon him. And Hathor kept him in the Field of Beans, where he still wanders, blindly, in his desire to seize the white feet of Queen Ahouri.

Ancestry

A S I looked at the key, it glinted in a long shaft of chalky light coming through a gap in the shutters. The small red wax seal still hung from it. It had been shut away for many years in the envelope which the lawyer had given me and which I had just opened. First I examined the death certificate; it seemed to me to be in order, written in French and English, and issued in an island of Oceania[1]. Nothing there to surprise me. I had never known my parents. The lawyer had acted as my guardian and through his good offices fees for the school which I formerly attended had been paid each year. The accompanying letter informed me that this key would open the small trunk of oriental wood which contained my family papers.

I had some difficulty finding it. I had no recollection of seeing the apartment I now visited and each of my movements released a cloud of dust and mould.

---

1 A geographic region which includes Australasia, Melanesia, Micronesia and Polynesia.

The lock on the trunk was of silver and iron and the light beam from the window lit it in the same way as it did the key. As soon as I opened it a wooden lever and a ring of woven straw fell into my hands. Then my fingers encountered phials of strong perfume, almost all evaporated. At the bottom was a package of papers: my inheritance.

They were stamped documents from consulates in Pacific islands; so I was convinced that I came from a family of seafarers. The names and entries had been countersigned. They had official stamps, so they seemed to have been issued by special institutions such as prisons or hospitals. There is no point in my revealing the names shown on these documents: they are the names of my grandfather, my great-grandfather and my great-great-grandfather. Each certificate showed the date and place of their death. My great-great-grandfather had died in 1785, my great-grandfather in 1811; my grandfather in 1849. I was struck by one thing: the three death certificates had been sent from Polynesia and drawn up on the northern coasts of the islands.

I have never had either illusions or qualms. In addition, the activities of my ancestors held no interest for me. If my curiosity was piqued it was because of the particular circumstances in which I found myself. Looking again at the death certificate my guardian had just sent me it was easy to ascertain that my father too had died on the north coast of a Polynesian island. Had my ancestors been settlers on the islands since 1785? Or what strange compulsion had led them to end their lives in the Pacific Ocean for the past four generations?

They could have been (I had thought) ship owners or captains, and with trade leading them towards dangerous reefs, they could have perished in shipwrecks. But four shipwrecks? My mind refuses to consider such a series of events. They could have been (I have no qualms about this) criminals or deportees. But four similar crimes, four identical sentences, the same deportation destination?

I could not envisage that they had, in fact, originated from those countries, or that they had been settled there since the eighteenth century. On the one hand, my family name did not indicate anything of that sort; on the other, how did I come to be in Europe, in France? How had I not received titles to property, inventories of farmlands?

None of these suppositions held water. I picked up the papers again and examined them afresh. The official stamps were illegible. The oldest, from 1785, was five-sided, printed in red ink. There were three letters left of the heading:

L E P . . .

The rest had disappeared.

*21 September 189**

One of my strangest ideas these past few days. Leprosy is endemic on all the northern coasts of the Polynesian islands. This matched the three letters of the red five-sided stamp. I shall go to see the lawyer.

The lawyer doesn't know anything. After consulting his files he showed me the guardianship deeds.

My father left for Polynesia at the age of thirty. Nothing appears about my grandfather or great-grandfather. A terrible anxiety has gripped me. I shall be thirty on 13 December. But firstly, nothing proves that leprosy is hereditary, nor that it appears in children at the same age as in the parents. Such madness! Nothing proves that my ancestors were lepers. What an imagination.

25 September 189*

I went to see a doctor. I asked him to examine me; I told him I was afraid of developing leprosy. The doctor laughed in my face. He's never seen leprosy. He doesn't know anything. Nobody knows anything. But I am calmer now. We are not governed by fate. I don't have to develop leprosy. Why should I alone be struck, amidst European societies, by a barbaric disease?

15 October 189*

I have broken the mirrors in my house. The walls can't watch me. I don't want to go out any more. I don't want anyone to look at my face! Now I'm going to calm down. For the past two weeks I have examined my face every morning. A little red spot on my forehead has filled me with fear.

This time I'm sure I have got my life under control. I am swaddled up to the chin in an undershirt of fine canvas. When my servant brings me food I order him to wait outside until I have put on my white mask. Nobody is going to see me, not even I myself. I shall get no warning.

13 December 189*

I'm thirty years old. I cannot resist this childish curiosity. I shall unpick the sleeve of my undershirt. From my wrist to my elbow there is a small irregular stripe of a chalky colour. It can't be true! It's not leprosy! I am not subject to this horrible law! I'm free, I'm free!

The Maison Close[1]

IT was a strange-looking house, closed, grey, its windows seeming to blink as it settled to sleep alongside a sloping street. The door was broken open, whitish and silent, with no lock, no doorbell and no knocker. It looked as if it had previously had on it the two-foot-high red cross with the legend: "The Lord have mercy upon us", as a warning that plague was inside. Or perhaps Morgiane[2] had marked it with chalk, long ago, to deceive the brigands. But time had worn away the words; the faint stains on the whitish wood no longer indicated plague, or wrongdoing; and that door seemed walled in silence.

The windows were hidden by day and night behind uniformly closed shutters. Even in really hot weather, when we pushed our fingers into the openings of the grooves we could feel cold air as if it were given off by the darkness inside the house. Sometimes during storms when the rain splashed down on the pavement

---

1 Literally "closed house" but also usually has the meaning of "brothel" in French.
2 The servant of Ali Baba in the *One Thousand and One Nights*.

two shutters would open as if to breathe in the storm and a red curtain would flutter in the deep darkness of an unknown bedroom.

And during the daytime the house was terribly silent. Neither the milk seller nor the postman knocked on the door in the morning. It was situated in such a way that it resembled that city in Upper Egypt, Syene[1], where no shadows were thrown at midday on the day of the summer solstice. For its walls blocked out the light of the sun; and at night it was completely wrapped in darkness.

There was a story that some children, having been knocking for a long time on the white door, had sat down to wait. Suddenly there was the sound of dreadful swearing inside. Then silence. And despite banging on the door with fists and feet, despite the mud and sand they threw against the shutters, they heard nothing more.

The lights in the house followed a regular pattern. Thus around nine in the evening a reddish light filtered through one of the shutters. At midnight it went out, and an hour later a jumble of yellow lamps could be seen. Precisely at daybreak all the lights disappeared.

We thought the house must be occupied by money forgers, and we tried to keep watch on it. But we never saw anyone coming out, or going in. And yet, they would need crucibles, metal, plaster and moulds, as well as accomplices to dispose of all the new coins.

And so we dreaded the closed house, without knowing anything. One night we stopped in front of it. At

---

1 Now Aswan.

a distance, from the edge of the pavement, we could hear the distinct sound of strong, regular, continual breathing, seeming to come out of the wall. It was as if some powerful sleeper was stretched along the inside of the wall. For more than an hour we listened to his breathing. And suddenly we fled, having imagined that the white door might open and that something would throw itself upon us.

The closed house, instead of giving shade from the sun, absorbed the sunlight. The house could not have been more silent, nor its white door more mute, if lepers had lived there. Gradually we took in this idea. We passed in front of the shutters, terrified of unexpectedly seeing a fleshless hand emerge. We held our breath as we crossed the road, so as not to inhale horrid unhealthy vapours. We would wake in our beds (for our house was more or less next door) hearing the sound of bells or wooden rattles[1]. Having read that lepers in earlier times had shut themselves away, wearing pale hoods and carrying two pieces of wood attached to a strap of woven straw, we became convinced that they sounded their knell in the night.

Once during a torrential rainstorm beating down in a single noisy sheet we saw a face behind the red billowing curtain. It was not a leper's face. It was the face of a small sickly girl with golden hair. She was weeping and shivering under the gusts of wind. When she caught sight of us she pulled an ugly face and shouted insults. But a hand pulled her back and pushed the shutters to.

---

1 As carried by lepers in the Middle Ages to warn of their presence.

During the night we were woken by a grinding noise. Then there were shouts and a crashing of furniture and broken glass. We got up and, half-dressed, slipped outside. There were now several lights on in the closed house and they were not following their usual pattern. A red lamp came on after a yellow lamp; another yellow lamp was moving quickly away from another window; behind one shutter a reddish glow was turning slowly.

And amid these lights coming on and off we could hear terrified moans and hiccupping sobs. Horrified, we rushed to the white door and bravely knocked loudly on it. There were two long moans like the sighs of a dying person. Then silence returned, the usual heavy silence. Then the lights went out one by one, not all together as they had at daybreak. All our shouts remained unanswered.

We went back to bed until dawn. Then as red streaks crossed the sky we opened the window. One of the shutters of the closed house was hanging open. We quickly went downstairs. By the light of the rising sun the small golden-haired girl was laughing. She laughed without replying to our questions. I took hold of her little hand; it was dirty, and under the nails were streaks of blood.

But by the time we had notified the police the little girl had disappeared; the closed house was found to be completely empty, clean, with no furniture, and the policemen, pointing out to us a "*For rent*" sign fixed to the white door, laughed in our faces.

The Life of Morphiel
A Demiurge[1]

MORPHIEL, like the other demiurges, was called into existence by the word of the Supreme Being who named him. He straightaway found himself in the same celestial workshop as Sar, Tor, Arochiel, Taouriel, Pthahil and Barokhiel. The demiurge in chief who ruled this workshop was Avathar. They were all working on constructing the world according to the preordained design. Avathar gave Morphiel his share of earth, water and metal; then he instructed him to create hair. The others were modelling noses, eyes, mouths, arms and legs. Barokhiel was concerned with making monstrosities, and deformed some of the finished objects before passing them to his foreman, Avathar. Some of the demiurges had actually worked on higher worlds and it was appropriate that this one should be different. And it was in following Avathar's invention that Barokhiel separated the nature of the men from that

---

1 A name for the Maker of the world in Platonic philosophy; in the Gnostic system, as here, conceived as subordinate to the Supreme Being and sometimes as the author of evil.

of the women, who, according to Plato, in the world immediately above ours formed a single being, walking on four feet and four hands arranged in a circular shape like the claws of a crab. There is an island in the world below where Avathar had men placed who had been divided once more. They have only one eye, one ear and one leg, and their brain is not separated in two but completely round. And what is even with us is uneven with them. For they are designed like monocotyledons[1] or those living tubes which attach themselves to rocks in the sea; and they have no concept of a second dimension in space, but think that the universe occurs intermittently at intervals. So hopping around on their one leg they easily cross what seems impenetrable to us—walls or mountains—and they count one, three, five, seven. Nor do they make love in twos; they can't imagine such a thing; instead they cling to each others' mouths in threes, fives or sevens, in small groups, gaining enormous pleasure; and they believe they can see their gods through holes in their sky. And the animals on this island are made the same way, and also the plants; so much so that only hopping can be seen, and solitary stems with a single rolled leaf; and all that is the creation of the diligent demiurges.

The demiurges' models were made with precious materials which were also used to create other universes, such as ether, subtle fire, diamond vapour; and it was in imitation of these models that everything on this earth was made; but Avathar did not allow his workers to use materials other than earth, water and metal. Several of

1 Flowering plants whose seeds have a single seed leaf, or cotyledon.

them, having been used to more intricate work, had more delicate feelings and objected. Avathar silenced them, and went from one to the other, carefully watching the movements of their hands. One must also assume that there were great jealousies amongst all these workers. Those who were creating the elite parts thought highly of themselves, like master porcelain makers; on the other hand, those who had been given the lower orders envied their more fortunate comrades and went unwillingly about their work of humble potters. Thus those who were making navels and toenails never ceased grumbling as their work progressed. Yet again, those who polished, shaped and coloured the pupils of eyes despised the other workers. As for Morphiel, he patiently carried out Avathar's instructions, drawing out both fine and thick hair.

Thus passed the life of Morphiel, the demiurge. It was rather like that of the prisoners labouring in a prison workshop under the eye of a warder. There was no variety. As soon as the Supreme Being had decided on a creation, the gods themselves were subject to the laws of those they were creating. Although vital craftsmen, they experienced the trials and the monotony of the existence of workers of the lower orders. During the time that Morphiel worked as a demiurge nothing worth mentioning happened to him.

But it happened that he fell in love with his work and skilfully put to one side the most beautiful of the hair he had made, without Avathar's knowledge. When the work on the creation of this world was finished, the demiurges were put to work on another project. In the new universe that they were constructing, there was no hair. Morphiel was thus free to wander off, and he took away with him the hair he had stolen. It was very beautiful hair, smooth and golden, long and soft, which Morphiel loved to touch.

Now, the new world which the demiurges were making was a world of male and female demons, made like men except that they had crests and combs instead of hair. One of the female demons, Everto, noticed the burden Morphiel was carrying. And wanting it, she took out of it what she needed to decorate her head with a woman's hair. Morphiel looked at her, and Everto caressed him in such a way that he did not dare to take back her adornment. Because the demiurges are in no way perfect. Everto relaxed with Morphiel for a while; then, like the real demon she was, she slipped off to earth where no one could tell her apart from other women. She paraded her smooth golden hair every-where, and the poor men caressed her and allowed themselves to be caressed as the demiurge had done. And the female demon Everto became famous among women, and brought to bear all her wickedness and evil-doing, so that the watchful gods became worried and made a report.

Avathar was immediately summoned and sent to find Morphiel, so that he could be punished. Morphiel was looking after his treasure, like a miser, in a lower world. Avathar seized him by the nape of the neck and hanged him from one of the gates of heaven with the hair he had made and loved. Such was the end of the guilty demiurge.

Towards Utopia

CYPRIEN D'ANARQUE was about forty years old. He would not have been pleased to be reminded of that. He claimed that his age was no more important to him than anything else in the world. Long-legged, lean and suntanned, he had a fierce gaze and a sharp face in which his frequent smiles showed two dimples at the corners of his mouth. He was a great reader of theories and did not tolerate contradictions; he was one of those who made a religion of believing in what they say at the moment they say it, a religion which has only one follower and which is enough for him. Cyprien's faith had become an obsession. He had such a pure admiration for his own ego that it would sicken him to contaminate it through contact with another ego; I mean, with any feeling, wish, idea, or word which was not exclusively Cyprienic. Far from wanting to resemble great men in some familiar detail (a fairly widespread ambition) he rejected any resemblance with horror. He had fallen out with his d'Anarque family in order to avoid any family likeness. He could not tolerate being found to have any analogy with another human being.

To start with, he had been interested in art, but only in art which seemed to have no relationship with any recognised school. Thus he began by admiring half-a-dozen painters, some of them unknown; others of whom people knew only one picture; others again, like the Master of the Female Half-Lengths[1], whose names we don't even know. He knew that in the grand hall of the Haarlem museum, below the panel showing the Brotherhood of St John of Jerusalem, a small door opens as if by magic, and that in a secret chamber can be seen a wonderful Saint Cecilia. In Paris he was familiar with a Descent from the Cross by Wohlgemuth, two portraits by Cranach, one by Fra Filippo Lippi, but he did not share this knowledge with anyone other than the owners of the works. In certain chapels in Germany he was the only one to have discovered the hand of Schoorl or of Schäuffelin on altarpieces that no one had looked at for four hundred years.

Unfortunately, his secrets, which he had thought were his alone to revere, were invaded one by one and revealed to the public by the curiosity of travellers, scholars conducting their research, or museum cataloguers.

So then he thought about writing, jealously keeping his manuscripts, copied on velum with a golden quill, under lock and key. Poetry had seemed to him more appropriate for a unique interlacing of rhythms and words. His work was thus composed of huge volumes

---

1 The name given to an unidentified Flemish painter or painters of the sixteenth century.

where the normal order of sentences was overturned, and in which the sentences themselves were composed as far as possible of words which no other poet had included in his verses, arranged in a way that no one until then could have imagined. For a while Cyprien was satisfied with this distinctiveness; but as he went on reading he had found, here and there, and written long before, certain of his own thoughts, his sentences and often his most outrageous eccentricities. So that he decided that in writing there is always imitation, even if we don't realise it.

"In the end," said Cyprien to himself one day, "if I'm forced to resemble someone else, if I have to be the same subject of admiration as someone else, if willy-nilly I have to think like someone else, do I have to act like someone else? Am I not free? And if my family, if people like me, even if circumstances combine to make me like someone else, can I not resist that, and be really myself?"

That was what was preoccupying Cyprien the very morning that his lady friend Musaraigne came to fetch him as lunchtime approached.

Cyprien d'Anarque was sitting at his empty table where he had arranged some new five-franc pieces, all exactly the same. He was concentrating on picking one without being able to fathom the motive for his choice. This worked when the coin was not particularly lit by a ray of sunshine, nor closer than any of the others, nor placed in some predestined order such as one, three or seven. But equally, none of these considerations should have led Cyprien not to choose a particular coin, but its neighbour. This delicate operation had had only one happy result during the morning; and Cyprien was smoking a cigar to have a break after this outcome when Musaraigne entered.

"Musaraigne," cried Cyprien, "don't move. You see these five-franc pieces. Take one."

"Done," said Musaraigne. "Is that all there is to do?"

"It's not such easy work," said Cyprien, "It's exhausted me. Why did you take that particular coin?"

"I don't know," said Musaraigne. "Why? Is it marked?"

"No, precisely not," replied Cyprien, "it's the same as the others, and that's what's extraordinary. Come on now, think about it, try to remember . . ."

"You're boring me," said Musaraigne. "Let's go and have lunch. I took it because I took it, that's all. God, you and your obsessions, it's unbearable! You have a new one every day."

"This child," said Cyprien to himself, "has freedom of action as she has of speech; by freedom I mean that she is unaware of her motives; she is free through ignorance. But for me, that's scarcely enough."

And he looked at her with admiration.

Lili Jonquille, or rather Musaraigne, was twenty years old and had no back story. Her face was just a small triangle of pale mobile flesh, cunning, inquisitive. Gold-coloured eyes; small hands like claws; a sinuous physique like flowing water, and nimble lips when she spoke. She read serialised stories, wept at all the dramas, didn't believe in medicine or politics, admired revolutionaries and those in authority simultaneously, adored comedians, knew by heart all the songs of the Montmartre night clubs, and one evening had even stood in for her friend Cigale at the Casino des Trottins[1]. Her credulity matched her scepticism; she was at the same time very vulnerable and very tough, very pitiful and very cruel. It was a case of the moment in time and the people she was dealing with. Thus she tended to believe all the tittle-tattle of her friend Cigale, but shrugged her shoulders at the smallest explanation on the part of Cyprien. She became indignant about certain criminals in the news, but expressed loud admiration for others who got themselves "gallantly" guillotined, without any clear rationale. She loved crayfish, game, rabbit and salad, very frothy champagne and fried food. She claimed to be able to recognise good mushrooms and certain trademarks. She disparaged "department stores" because "their prices were high to cover the cost of their window displays". And yet she had confidence in some fashionable suppliers who in fact were not distinguished for their cheapness. Finally, she had a horror of hospitals, the police, spiders and magistrates; but she would not miss going to see the President of the Republic pass by.

Musaraigne despised Cyprien and adored him. She disdained him because he did not understand slang, and adored him because he didn't understand it. Disdain is an indication of a certain discord. As is adoration. Cyprien did not disdain Lili because she preferred a new hat to the most beautiful fourteenth-century *cas-*

---

1 Young women working part-time as prostitutes.

soni[1], but he didn't adore her, thinking he understood her too well.

However, this time he did not understand her with his usual infallibility. He had come, little by little, to the conclusion that the highest point of difference between him and his counterparts was the total freedom in the exercise of his personality. And now he, Cyprien d'Anarque, had arrived at this point only with the greatest difficulty, whilst this young girl, at the first go, had arrived there just like that!

Cyprien was in this state of perplexity when Ambroise Babeuf came in.

Ambroise Babeuf looked oddly like a mushroom with two shiny specks of eyes. He had studied history for a long time, and was convinced that historical methods were not scientific. First he had collected facts from memoirs, newspapers and correspondence, following Taine's[2] methodology to extract general laws. Then he was seized with doubt about how to interpret these facts. For they all came from third parties or they were personal souvenirs noted twenty years later, or they were gleaned from letters: but a letter is addressed to someone, and do people always tell the truth? So that finally Babeuf reached a point where he only had confidence in authenticated materials: receipts, wills, registers of births and deaths, judicial reports, legal certificates. But now a new difficulty emerged. These

---

1 Rich Italian-style chests which may be inlaid or elaborately carved.

2 Taine (1828-1893) was a critic and historian who applied scientific methods to the study of history, philosophy and aesthetics.

documents prove that it is true that at a certain date the man being studied was in a certain place, was of a certain age, that he had received a certain sum of money and that he possessed certain assets. But they don't allow us to get to know the man himself, and the historian is not in a position to describe him nor what he was thinking. At this precise point Ambroise Babeuf entered the picture, and the man he was describing was shown according to the image Babeuf had himself constructed. At that point too, the science stopped. For Babeuf did not trust Babeuf and refused to make himself the criterion by which he judged the truth of history.

At this period of his life Babeuf, disappointed by history but still having confidence in facts, tended to reply when asked about his next book:

"I'm not writing any more. If you want to make me happy, give me the *Dictionnaire des Postes*[1] to copy onto index cards. At least there I'll have some certainty. Yes, let's make index cards."

The hope that a precise knowledge of his own mind would one day allow him to interpret facts scientifically had led Ambroise to psychology, and very rapidly from there, through seeking a solid foundation, to anatomy and physiology, particularly of the brain. What was the basis for thoughts? Was it brain cells? By what process did the cells, which seemed very marginally differentiated, receive impressions, store memories, construct

---

1 A directory of all the towns, villages and communities in France first published in the eighteenth century.

imagination, willpower, rationality? So that Babeuf spent the day in his laboratory cutting up brains and examining pieces under a microscope. He had a perfect knowledge of the histology of all areas of the brain and the structure of the cells. But a cell was no more help than a signed certificate or a receipt in revealing the truth. It was a fact that gave nothing away about personality. Could you break it down, go further? Maybe; but Babeuf had convinced himself that the science of the human body, like the science of human facts, had its limitations. And he would repeat:

"We'll not find anything. We'll never find anything. But you have to cut up brains. Yes, let's keep working; let's cut up the brains."

"Babeuf," cried Cyprien, "do you really think I'm free?"

"My friend," said Babeuf, "that's not impossible. We sometimes see some strange malformations. One of our leading surgeons has just operated on a perfect hermaphrodite: which proves that at least once nature wasn't able to make a distinction. Monsieur Boussinesq[1], who is a learned physician, has proved that in certain conditions liquids seem to move of their own accord, outside the laws of equilibrium. Monsieur Boutroux[2], an accomplished philosopher, believes that the laws of the universe are not immutable. And the observations of astronomers of light from the stars show that space, where the planets spin, does not conform exactly to

1 Joseph Boussinesq, 1842-1929, a mathematician.
2 Emile Boutroux, 1845-1921, a philosopher and university teacher with whom Schwob studied.

geometrical space; there may be more than three dimensions, or fewer. If geometry is not infallible, why would you Cyprien not be free? Besides, what does your liberty matter? You'd be an anomaly, that's all. It would be better to know all the laws and their meanings. Yes, you see, we have to work; it's not likely that we'll ever find anything; but let's work anyway, let's cut up brains."

"No," said Lili, "let's go and have lunch."

"Musaraigne is right," said Cyprien. "Let's have lunch first; I'll respond afterwards, unless we chat about something else."

www.ingramcontent.com/pod-product-compliance
Lightning Source LLC
Chambersburg PA
CBHW050149110726

47898CB00008B/2723